Fatal
Obsession

By

USA Today
Bestselling Author

CASI MCLEAN

Fatal Obsession

This is a work of fiction. Names, characters, places, and incidents are either the product of the author's imagination or are used fictitiously, and any resemblance to actual persons living or dead, business establishments, events, or locales, is entirely coincidental.

ISBN: 9798477035106

Contact Information: casi@casimclean.com

Cover Art by Margret Daly and Ada Frost
Editing & Proofreading by Linda Carroll-Bradd

To get the latest news about her writing and art: Subscribe to her Newsletter on casimclean.com & Follow her on Amazon and BookBub!

Dedication

Fatal Obsession is dedicated to my son, Andrew, who's love for NFL football inspired me to broaden my horizons.

.

Praise For Casi McLean

"Masterfully Written! Fatal Obsession' by Casi McLean is the new taut thriller from the pen of this multi-genre author. This character-driven novel plays cleverly with the points of view of the protagonists and antagonists, allowing the reader into the mind of the latter as he implements his plan. The novel bounces off unforeseen twists that create tension and anxiety, enveloping the reader in the uncomfortable situation. Readers will experience a masterful piece of writing from this acclaimed author. —**Enrico Graffiti**

"I've loved everything I've read from this award-winning author. Fatal Obsession is a fast-paced psychological thriller with a bunch of twists and turns that will keep you guessing until the very end. If you enjoy romantic suspense thrillers with quality writing, not to mention engaging, well-developed characters, this book is a must read for you!!" — **Tammy**

"Casi McLean delivers a fast-paced, gripping tale of deception in her thriller, Fatal Obsession. The book is paced perfectly and doesn't bog you down with unnecessary details that you find in many thrillers like this one. if you love romantic suspense and thrillers, then you'll love Fatal

Obsession. With the twists and turns hidden in this book, you'll need to keep turning the pages to find out the secrets brought into the light. I highly recommend Fatal Obsession if you love quality romantic suspense with engaging, real-life characters you can relate to." — **Sugar**

"This is the first Casi McLean novel I've read. Great character building and wonderful writing. I fell in love with the main characters immediately, and McLean even coaxed a little sympathy out of me for the protagonist at the end. It's nicely paced, unique plot, and superb dialect." — **Cyndie Zahner**

"Fatal Obsession delivers a spine-tingling psychological thriller, dangerous secrets, revenge, murder and like the title says obsession. If you like your thrillers with a side of nonstop action, heart pounding twists and turns you won't see coming, you don't want to miss Fatal Obsession by Casi McLean! I highly recommend it!" — **Tena Stetler**

"I love this kind of thriller, and Fatal Obsession delivers the best. Dangerous secrets, obsession, revenge, murder, and the best elements of psychological thriller are just the beginning of this white-knuckle stunner. The story is unputdownable, full of nonstop, spine-tingling twists, turns and surprises that you won't see coming. I enjoy psychological thrillers, this one will leave you gasping. Well done and fabulous – five stars!" — **JA Schneide**

Fatal Obsession

Prologue

Shoes clapping against the cold linoleum floor, Daryl Quinn walked room to room, making sure he hadn't left a single shred of evidence he'd ever lived in this dump. He smiled at how his footsteps echoed through the emptiness. Opening the front door, he paused and scanned the great room one last time. "Good riddance," he grumbled and slammed the door behind him. Never again would he have to spend another night in this hellhole.

Most people would feel a tug of sentimentality at leaving their childhood home, but not Daryl. The pale gray walls had closed in

1

on him since his momma's death and, after two years, her dying words still haunted him. Now, he would finally have revenge.

Chapter One

Thursday Evening, February 25—Day Five QB
NFL Combine,
Indianapolis, Indiana

Lowering his head, Deke Madigan leaned a hand against the wall and closed his eyes while warm water cascaded through his sweat-dampened hair and swathed his naked body. "Nailed it." He'd never worked harder for anything in his life and left nothing on the table. Adrenaline still pumping his muscles, he stretched his neck to one side, then, the other to loosen the tension.

"Great workout, Deke. You're a lock for a first-round draft pick." Matt chuckled, his voice echoing through the empty locker room.

Peering under his arm to see his friend, Deke raised a brow. "You're hangin' right there with me, buddy." He straightened, reached for the soap dispenser, and pressed a glob onto his palm.

"I wish. Seriously, bro, you've been golden all season. Winning the Heisman in December. Convincing Elise Sloan to marry you on Valentine's Day. And now this? You slayed the entire NFL Combine." He shook his head. "Whatever you're drinking, save some for me."

Deke raised an arm and slathered soap under his pit, then onto his chest. "It's called working your ass off."

"Ha. You better save some of that ass for your hot fiancée." He glanced at his watch. "I'm outta here. My interview starts in a half hour."

"Damn, I had no idea it was that late."

"As usual, you're the last to leave, Deke. I'll catch you later." He turned and paced toward the door.

"Hey, Matt," Deke hollered. "You've got this. Kick ass."

He called over his shoulder, "I plan to. Later, buddy." The door slammed behind him.

Deke pressed a few squirts of shampoo onto his hand and scratched his fingernails through his hair. The suds slid over his face, and he rubbed them into the stubble around his mouth and chin. Matt was right. The last few months, Deke's life had played out like a dream come true. Winning the Heisman not only fulfilled a childhood fantasy, the trophy created a springboard toward a prime NFL pick.

His mind swirled to thoughts of Elise and the look on her face when the Heisman Trophy

Trust announced Deke as the winner. If he had to choose between an NFL career he'd spent years working to attain and having Elise in his life, he'd be seriously torn. When he met her, he won the lottery. The sight of her running across the football field straight toward him, a microphone gripped in her hand, was etched in his mind.

The game against South Carolina was tied. But with twenty-three seconds left in the fourth quarter, Deke threw a Hail Mary right into Hershel's arms in the end zone. After the game, he gave a few interviews, then jogged toward the locker room, until he saw Elise from the corner of his eye. Her long, deep-brown hair, crystal-blue eyes, and a beautiful, dimpled smile mesmerized him the first time their gazes met. And her love for football iced the cake. She had a body guys fantasized about and a no-nonsense personality that set her apart from any girl Deke had ever known. Smart, sexy, thoughtful. An intense heat swirled into his groin at the thought of her soft, pink lips pressing against his.

How his dream woman fell for him had him thanking God every day. He couldn't imagine a more perfect wife. Remembering he'd promised to call her after the workout tonight, he picked up his pace, lathered his legs and feet, then stepped into the rain-shower to rinse off.

Thoughts on Elise, he barely heard the click of a locker closing behind him. His mind drifted between Elise and wondering where he'd land after the draft played out, until the hairs on his neck rose. He sensed someone watching him and spun to see a water-blurred image only a few feet away. Rubbing his eyes to see more clearly, he stared, but his mind refused to accept who he saw. "What the hell?"

In a blink, an arm wrapped around his neck and a hand clamped over his mouth. The chokehold pressed against his neck. Soaking wet and completely unprepared, he couldn't react—couldn't counterpunch—couldn't breathe. Again, Deke flashed on his assailant's face in utter confusion, until his surroundings faded, blackness enveloped him, and he slid into a deep, dark abyss.

When a soft, purring hum vibrated next to her ear, Elise Sloan rolled over and buried her head under her pillow. But the sound refused to silence. Instead, the whir intensified until it grew into an intolerable droning noise. Now, awake enough to realize the abrasive whine emanated from her phone, she forced open her eyelids and shot a groggy gaze toward the clock. Six twenty-three a.m. Who on Earth would call her this early? She ran a hand through her pillow-scraggly hair and rubbed her eyes. Snatching her cell from the side table, she stared at the number. A cold chill bristled down her back. Pressing Accept, she shifted her weight onto an elbow.

"Matt? What's wrong? Is Deke hurt?"

"Damn, Elise, are you psychic?"

"No, you just never call unless it's an emergency." She tightened her grip on the phone.

"Right." He paused and drew in an audible breath.

"What happened? Was he injured during his workout?"

"No, nothing like that. He's okay, but he was involved in some kind of…a skirmish."

"Oh, God. I worried something was wrong when he didn't call last night. How is he? Do I need to come—"

"Slow down and take a breath, Elise. I haven't seen him yet, but the coach said it looks like he was in a struggle of some kind…or maybe mugged."

"Mugged? Why? I mean, how could that even happen? Deke said security was tight. Besides, why would anyone want to mug Deke? It's not like he carries a lot of money to the workouts."

"I know. All great questions, and I don't have any answers, at least, not yet. The last time I saw him, he was showering in the locker room. He had a helluva workout, and I figured he'd go back to his room and crash."

"Who found him, and where? Was he still in the locker room?"

"That's the strange thing. Security found him wandering the concessions at street level around ten last night. The coaches informed us around eleven p.m. They said Deke doesn't remember what happened, but he had bruises on his neck and was disoriented."

"Is he in the hospital?"

"Nah. The NFLPS physicians whisked him away for observation. They're the best, Elise. They gave us all thorough exams before we could participate in the workouts." A long moment of silence ensued before he continued. "They haven't told us anything else. I just thought you should know."

"Thanks." She sat up straight and leaned against the headboard. "This might sound like a conspiracy theory, but do you think someone…I mean, what if one of the competitors wants him out of the competition?" A knot fisted in the pit of her stomach as she considered the possibility. "I've interviewed a lot of great quarterbacks this season." She bit the corner of her lower lip. "What if one of them decided his chances would increase dramatically if Deke was injured?"

"Damn, Elise. You could be right. The competition here is brutal. And after today's workout, Deke definitely tops the QB list for number one draft pick."

"I never mentioned the idea to Deke, for obvious reasons, but I have to admit, the thought crossed my mind more than once. What if some desperate competitor—or someone close to one like a coach—targeted Deke? If they hurt him or take him out of play, other contenders rise to the top."

"That sounds a lot more reasonable than a mugging. I wonder if the coaches considered the possibility." He paused a long beat. "But Deke was right about the security around here, it's hard to believe someone could walk in off the street."

"I just hope he's okay."

"The docs wanted to watch him for a few hours. He might be back in his room already. Although, I tried to call him a few times, but my calls went straight to voicemail. Still, he doesn't take his cellphone to workouts. Maybe his phone is dead or in his suitcase. I'm sure he'll be okay."

"Yeah. That makes sense." She slid down into her covers. "Thanks for calling, Matt. I know he'll contact me when he can, but will you please let me know if you hear anything else?"

"Of course. And feel free to call me if you don't hear from him soon."

"Fingers crossed I won't need to." She pressed End and dropped her phone onto her lap.

Thoughts spinning, she snuggled back into bed and drew the covers to her neck. As a fledgling sportscaster, she'd been trained to probe beyond surface information. She couldn't help but question who might have targeted Deke. She stared at the ceiling, her curiosity flying into overdrive with myriad what-if scenarios, until dawn crept through the window and cast eerie shadows across the bedroom.

With a sudden thud, an intense weight crushed against her stomach and chest, followed by a series of slobbery licks across her face. "Geez, Jaz. I've got to teach you a gentler way to wake me." She gave the golden retriever pup a strong hug, then ushered him off the bed and shot a gaze at the time, six forty-eight. "I guess it's time to get up." She scratched Jasper's head. "Let me throw on some clothes, then I'll take you out, okay, boy?"

She ambled into the bathroom to start her day. It wouldn't hurt to get to work a little early. Fridays were always busy, especially when she covered a nighttime basketball game, like tonight. And her lunch date with Britt would take a bit out of her time. For that, she was thankful, though. Brittney Gordon had been Elise's best friend forever. They'd known each other since childhood, and they were practically joined at the hip. Both with long brown hair and a similar build, they looked like sisters, if not twins... except Britt had emerald-green eyes and Elise's were blue. Now that she and Britt landed career-oriented jobs, they had little girl-time together. She looked forward to bouncing off her concern over Deke's attack with Britt. As a DNA crime scene analyst, Britt was in a much better position to give Elise an objective point of view.

Chapter Two

The NFL Combine participants stayed at The Crown Plaza Hotel, located on West Louisiana Street in Indianapolis, adjacent to the Convention Center and the Lucas Oil Stadium where they performed workouts. The Combine provided breakfast, lunch, and dinners in various locations and times, depending on the day's activities, and sports nutritionists created menus to maximize performance. But if players missed scheduled meals, hotel room service and dining were offered on a cash-only basis, and each player was responsible to foot his own bill. Deke made sure he didn't miss a meal—even if he felt like shit.

Tanner Wells pushed open the hotel room door. "Last call for breakfast, Deke. You comin'?"

He rolled over and eyed his roommate, then glanced at his watch. "Damn. I didn't get a bit of sleep last night with the doctors hovering over me. I just got back to the room. Why the hell can't we get lunch through room service?"

"Rules are rules."

He harrumphed. "Right." He rolled to his side. Dragging his feet around, he hung them over the side of the bed and hauled himself into a sit. "My entire body aches." Elbows on his knees, he dropped his throbbing head into his palms.

"Do you remember anything more about what happened last night?"

Lifting his gaze, he flattened his lips. "Nah. The whole evening is a blur. I remember showering, then nothing until I was wandering through the concession area."

Tanner shrugged. "Lucky you finished the program before you got jumped."

Pinching his brows together, Deke frowned. "Yeah. Lucky."

"I'm outta here this afternoon. You leaving tonight or tomorrow?"

Deke shot him a stare. "My flight leaves tomorrow night. I wanted to stick around and watch the final workouts."

"Well, it's been nice getting to know you, Deke." Tanner grasped his gym bag from his bed and slung it over his left shoulder, then held out a hand. "If I don't see you again before I leave for the airport, good luck with the draft."

"Yeah. You, too." Deke extended his right arm and gave him a firm shake.

When the door slammed behind his roommate, Deke stood and raked a palm through his hair, then padded toward the bathroom. He had a lot to do before his flight tomorrow night. Smiling, he thought about how hard he'd worked to get here.

He was a shoo-in for a first-round draft pick. All his diligence was finally paying off. He'd locked in his future, and he couldn't wait to get home to see Elise. He'd call her this morning, before he got too involved in the day's activities.

Glancing into the mirror, he inspected at his reflection, his thoughts swirling with uncharted plans of his future.

By the time Elise reached her office, it was almost eight o'clock. She'd just pulled into her parking spot when her phone buzzed. Expecting a call from Deke, she dug through her purse for her cell, then stared at the screen. "Thank God, Deke. I've been so worried. What happened last night. Matt called me and said—"

"Matt called you?"

"Yes, thank God."

"He shouldn't have worried you."

"I'm glad he did. What happened? Are you okay?"

"I'm fine. A little bruised and achy, but I'll live."

She breathed a long sigh of relief. "It's so good to hear your voice. Seriously, Deke. Do you know if the police have any suspects?"

13

"Not that I know of. I can't remember the incident at all. I was showering, then everything afterward went black."

She tapped her fingers on the console. How could he not remember anything? Why was he alone in the mezzanine at ten o'clock at night? And with security so strict, how could some random person get into the locker room and attack him without being seen? "But you're sure you are okay, physically?"

"Absolutely. So, did Matt tell you about my last workout, too?"

"Not really. He said you slayed it, but I knew you would." She smiled, imagining how he felt when he knew he killed the final workout.

"Well, I'll tell you more when I get home. I just wanted to let you know what time I'll be back. My flight lands at eight thirty Saturday night. I'm pretty sure I'll be spent, so I'll crash at my place. Are you free for brunch Sunday morning?"

"Sure." She slumped. Aware he'd be exhausted after the week-long ordeal, she couldn't help feeling a little disappointed he didn't want to rush home to see her the moment he landed.

"Good. How about Ray's on the River, at noon? I'll pick you up at eleven-thirty."

He obviously didn't want her to worry, and she wanted to sound upbeat. "Perfect. You know how much I love their Sunday brunch."

"I've gotta run to catch breakfast. I'll see you Sunday?"

"I can't wait." Her voice softened. "I miss you, Deke."

"Miss you, too, Elise. See you soon." He ended the call.

She lowered the phone and sat in silence for several minutes. Deke's tone seemed really edgy…but he'd been through a lot and had obviously slept very little. Shrugging off the thought, she grabbed her purse, locked her car, and strolled inside.

Chapter Three

The TV-5 Atlanta, Georgia—more commonly known as WAGA—building was nothing like a typical office, especially the construction. Situated atop a hill on Briarcliff Road, the structure looked more like Tara from Gone With The Wind and radiated the same elegance.

Elise loved the serene feeling she got every time she arrived or left. A huge porch, set in the middle of the structure, was accented by four dramatic white columns, and overlooked a lush, well-kept lawn with a circular driveway. And though the inside of the manor was renovated for office space, the grandeur still maintained the feel of an antebellum mansion.

By noon, Elise had put in a full day's work. Typical for a Friday, the newsroom buzzed, and she was thankful for a much-needed break. She closed her computer, grabbed her purse, and wandered down the hallway to the impressive spiral staircase that led to the lobby.

As she hustled outside toward her car, she paused and drew in a lungful of the crisp, cool air, then touched her key fob. When the door opened, she slid inside and pressed Start. Sitting in the driver's seat as the BMW roared to life still gave her a rush. She pulled out of the parking lot onto Briarcliff Road and headed toward Lenox Square, reminiscing. Elise loved this car the moment she laid eyes on it. Her dad purchased the new ice-blue convertible with cream interior and for years, she'd begged him to give her the car when she got her driver's license. Instead, he made her work for ownership and finally acquiesced when she graduated from University of Georgia.

By the time Elise arrived at The True Food Kitchen, Britt had already chosen a corner table by the window and sipped on a tall glass of cranberry limeade.

She motioned toward a duplicate drink sitting across from her. "Come. Sit."

Elise gave her a quick hug. "Thank you." She couldn't wait to sip one of her all-time favorite drinks. She hung her purse on the back of her chair and took a long swig before she sat. "Have you ordered lunch, yet?"

"Nope. I couldn't decide if I wanted the chicken avocado wrap, shrimp tacos, or salmon, and I thought you might have a preference after the morning you had."

"Thanks. I love everything here, but today, the avocado wrap sounds really good." She pulled in her chair, then leaned forward. "So, what do you think? Am I overreacting?"

"No. I was stunned when I got your text this morning."

"So, was Deke's attack a random hit, or do you think someone wants him out of the picture?"

For a beat, she twisted her lips to one side before answering. "First of all, I can't imagine anyone randomly entering the property. But even if they sneaked inside, arbitrarily encountering Deke in the shower and jumping him? No. That's too weird."

"I totally agree." Seeing the server approach, Elise leaned against the back of her chair.

"Good afternoon, ladies." Her long, blonde hair swept over her shoulders and covered her name tag. "I'm Caitlynn, and I'll be your server today. What can I bring you for lunch?"

"I'll have the avocado wrap," Elise spoke up.

She tapped something on her tablet, then shifted her gaze toward Britt. "And you, miss?"

"I'd like the shrimp tacos, please."

"Got it. If you need anything else, just let me know." She turned and paced toward the bar.

Britt took a sip of her drink, then continued the discussion. "Remember, we don't know the whole story. Don't worry too much, Elise. When Deke gets back in town, I'm sure he'll give you more details. Let's just enjoy lunch."

"You're right. At least, I know he's okay, and he'll be home tomorrow. He wants us to have brunch at Ray's on Sunday. I thought I'd run over to the mall after lunch. You want to come with?"

"Sure. Since I know I'll be wearing whatever you buy, I want to make sure you pick something I like." She chuckled.

After lunch, they strolled through the mall, popping into favorite stores along the way. Rummaging through a Neiman Marcus rack, Elise blankly gazed from one dress to the next. Though she wanted to find an outfit that would temporarily distract Deke from football, her thoughts wandered five hundred miles away.

Over the moon since Deke proposed, Elise wanted to be the most important thing in his life. And though she loved sports and realized she'd take a backseat to football for a while, she couldn't help but feel like an afterthought, at times. She drew in a long breath and pursed her lips.

Wait, what was she thinking? If she hadn't been covering the University of Georgia's game for Channel-Five News last year, she might not have even met Deke. She'd never forget that day. After he threw a Hail Mary into the endzone to win the game against University of South Carolina, Elise ran the entire length of the field through the crowd to catch him before he disappeared into the locker room.

Just as he was about to turn the corner, she yelled his name. She turned, and their gazes met. For an obscenely long minute, she forgot the interview—her reason for being there. Frozen by his ice-blue eyes staring into hers, and with a mic gripped tightly in hand, she couldn't breathe, let alone speak. But Deke deflected her embarrassment by placing a hand on her shoulder.

"You win. I'll give you an interview. But let's step to one side before we get trampled by this crazy crowd."

In that moment, he charmed her, and she knew she never wanted to stop gazing into those enchanting blue eyes.

"Let me see that one."

Her momentary trance broken, Elise turned toward her friend. "What?"

"The dress you're holding. Are you going to try it on? 'Cuz if you don't, I will."

Elise inspected the white gown now gripped in her hand. "I like this one." She held it close to her body and admired the ice-blue piping accenting the shimmering white. "What do you think?"

"I really like the draped neckline and the trim brings out your eyes." She ran a hand over the fabric. "Is it silk?"

Elise gazed at the tag. "No, a polyester blend, but it's really silky-smooth and I like the cut. I hope it fits." Again, she held it against her chest and, this time, peered into the wall mirror next to the rack. "Deke will love this one." She turned toward Britt. "I've got to try it on."

"Hang on." Britt returned her gaze to the gowns, plucked from the rack one she'd been eyeing, then draped it over her arm. "I'll try on this one." As they strolled to the fitting rooms, she nudged Elise's shoulder. "So, are you planning anything special to celebrate Deke's homecoming?"

Elise entered a stall and hung it on a hook. "I want to. He's been so focused on his workouts and performing his best for the scouts. I'd like to plan something different. You know? Like a fun event to get his mind off football and help him relax, for a change." She wiggled into her dress, then stood back and inspected her reflection.

"Why not surprise him with a weekend at your family's cabin at Lake Lanier?" Britt mused. She slid the drape aside and stuck her head into Elise's stall. "You could cook him dinner or pack a picnic lunch with finger foods and hike to the waterfalls. That would be so romantic." Britt sucked her lips together like a fish and flashed her lashes to emphasize the starry-eyed ambiance, then withdrew into her own stall.

"Ha, ha. Actually, I like that idea." When she fastened the clasp, Elise stepped out of the fitting room and stood in front of the three-way mirror. "What do you think?"

Again, Britt poked her head out of her dressing room. "Oh my gosh, Elise." She stepped from her stall and ogled her friend. "You have to buy it. That design was made for you, girl." Britt edged closer to the mirror and smiled. "Wow. Deke will absolutely…rip it off of you." She snickered.

"Sold." Elise turned toward Britt and chuckled. "I love your outfit."

Britt gazed downward at her bra and panties and rolled her eyes. "Right. The perfect imaginary gown for my non-existent boyfriend." She laughed and ducked into her dressing room.

"The love of your life will come, Britt. When you least expect him."

"That would be now." She shoved aside the drape and walked toward Elise, still fastening her pants, then gazed at her watch. "Damn. It's almost one-thirty. I need to get back to work. I told Dr. Hellman I had an errand to run and needed to take a long lunch. He said to take my time, but I don't want to push it. I really love this job."

Elise cringed. "The technology is amazing, but the thought of collecting and analyzing samples from violent crime scenes." She cringed. "I couldn't do that." A stream of prickles shot down her arms. To alleviate the sensation, she rubbed a hand over the chill bumps, then glanced at her watch. "I need to get going, too. I'm covering the Georgia Tech–Syracuse basketball game tonight. I have to be there by four thirty to prep for the seven-p.m. game, and I want to go over my notes before I leave." Considering the purchase, she stepped into her fitting room, slid into her jeans and t-shirt, then grabbed her things. "I really love this dress." Exiting the fitting room, she checked the price tag and frowned. "I might have to eat apples for lunch the next few weeks to afford it, though."

"Do it, Elise. It's gorgeous." Britt gave her a quick hug. "I have to run."

"Me, too, but I'm really glad we made time to catch up. Let's make plans to do this more often."

"Definitely. Muah," Britt mouthed a kiss. "I'll call you later." She spun and disappeared through the rows of clothes.

Elise gazed at the silky white gown. The cut accentuated all her assets, while hiding the little belly she'd tried forever to lose. She folded the frock over her arm and huffed. Why did she have champagne tastes with a beer budget?

After putting the dress on her ever-increasing credit card, Elise swung by the office. She read through her game notes, then tucked them into her satchel and made a quick call to Lance Keaton, her press photographer, to coordinate their plans for the evening. By two forty, she headed home to feed and walk Jasper. She parked and strolled toward her ground level condo but stopped cold when she noticed her deck door...ajar.

Chapter Four

Already spooked by Deke's attack, Elise edged closer to the entrance. Should she call 911? Maybe. But if she did, then found no signs of an intruder...no. Before alerting the police, she'd take a peek into the dining room. When she reached the porch, she pressed her back against the side wall and leaned toward the window to look inside. Seeing nothing more than the adjacent living room wall, she softly pushed open the door with her foot, then peered into the kitchen. Before her brain could register, she saw a flash. Jasper jumped forward and leapt into her arms, wiggling, and licking her face.

Still a bit shaken, she shook her head. "Okay, boy, settle down. I'm happy to see you, too." When she lowered him to the floor, she saw her neighbor standing in the kitchen, fists resting on her waist. She jerked, pressing her brows together, and frowned.

"I'm sorry, dear. I didn't mean to scare you. Jasper was barking like crazy—which he never does—do you, boy?" Mrs. Murphy bent over to pat his head. "He was so upset. I used your spare key so I could take him outside to piddle. I didn't want you to come home to a mess, hon. I hope that's okay."

"Of course. I gave you a copy of my key for emergencies, and Jasper needing to go out seems like just that." Elise shifted her gaze to her puppy.

"He's usually so quiet, but he was barking up a storm."

"I appreciate you taking care of him, Mrs. Murphy. Thank you."

"Now that you're home, I'll be on my way, dear. Have a nice evening." She stepped past Elise and ambled outside.

Elise turned toward Jasper. "I wonder what agitated you, boy. Did you see a squirrel rummaging around the porch?" She leaned over and gave him a scrunch behind his ear. "From now on, maybe I should close the curtains when I leave. We don't want to cause that sweet old lady to have a heart attack."

She snatched Jasper's leash from the counter and returned it to the hook inside the coat closet, then filled his bowl with kibble. Stepping toward her bedroom to change clothes and touch up her makeup, she couldn't stop her thoughts from drifting to Deke.

Three years his senior, Elise had felt like she'd robbed the cradle when they started dating. She kept reminding herself Deke was only a freshman at UGA the year she graduated, but her heart wouldn't let go. Professionally, she'd seen his rise to fame over the past few years as she covered her alma mater's games. was injured preseason, and Deke stepped into the big break he needed. He started game one with an explosive performance and never looked back. Oddly, that Georgia versus South Carolina game was the first time she'd interviewed Deke one on one, and their chemistry ignited.

The first time he asked her out, she said no, despite how his very presence shot hot tingles between her thighs. Not because of the age difference, although that excuse was her initial reason to turn him down. Her history with jocks was far from stellar. In her experience, the limelight did something evil to guys. Every athlete she dated ended up cheating. The last one asked her to marry him. She agreed to move in together, but one night, when she walked in on him *scoring* with a cheerleader after a game, their relationship abruptly ended. From that moment forward, Elise swore off jocks completely and hadn't so much as considered dating an athlete again—until Deke.

Turning down his first request to take her to dinner only strengthened his resolve. He respectfully pursued her, sending her a single white rose at work with a very sweet note and going out of his way to bump into her at the next game. The entire university knew his routine. Deke Madigan never dated during football season. And even in offseason, he avoided wild campus parties, cheerleaders, and groupies. Deke was unlike any athlete she'd ever known, and he definitely captured Elise's attention. When she finally agreed to a date, she swore to take things slowly, one day at a time. Surprisingly, Deke respected her decision. When he was with Elise, he never noticed other women. His focus was steadfast on her, not the female fans who shamelessly flirted with him. Elise was smitten with Deke. Every time she heard his voice, she got butterflies.

Once she agreed to that first date, she couldn't deny their chemistry. Their attraction was palpable, and she knew in her soul Deke would never cheat. When he asked her to marry him, she didn't hesitate. She loved this man with all her heart, and she knew he loved her. If anything happened to him...she drew in a deep breath and brushed off the thought. One thing she knew for sure, Deke could take care of himself.

After changing her clothes, Elise freshened up and got dressed for the evening, then returned to Jasper. Glancing at her watch, she closed the drapes, then flipped on the TV. "Maybe the sound will distract you from outside noises, buddy." Again, she gave Jasper an affectionate scrunch. "I'll be back in a while, boy. Be good." She grabbed her equipment and purse, wondering how silly it was to tell her dog she'd be home soon. Did he have a clue what she meant? Probably not, but she thought on some level he at least sensed the idea.

Slipping through the door, she twisted the lock, then closed it behind her and tilted her wrist to check her watch. Now running late, she picked up her pace to her car. To meet Lance on time, she'd need to hustle.

Sitting on a park bench about twenty yards behind Elise's Enclave condo, Daryl Quinn watched her rush across the parking lot to her car. He knew she intended to meet Lance Keaton, her cameraman. He also knew precisely where they would go and had a rough idea how long the game would last. But this time, her routine made little difference. His task here was almost complete.

Such a privileged bitch. She grew up in the lap of luxury. And her well-to-do daddy paid for her prissy car and pricey education. He harrumphed at the thought. He'd do her, though. In a heartbeat, and the time was near. So near he could smell it.

Now that he'd parked his rig in a secluded, secure spot, he'd drive a rental car for his return trip. An eight-hour drive was nothing for Daryl. After Elise pulled out of the parking lot, he returned to her apartment and slid a key into the lock, then slowly opened the door.

"Rrrrrrrrrr," Jasper growled, but this time a little less intimidating.

Daryl edged inside, then softly closed the door. Jasper was an unexpected in

"Rrrrrrrrrrr."

He bent over and offered the dog a treat he'd purchased to lure him. "Come on, boy. I won't hurt you unless you make me."

Jasper growled again, this time showing his teeth.

Tossing the treat forward, Daryl watched the dog sniff, then crunch and swallow the biscuit. "See, I'm not so bad once you get to know me." Digging into his pocket again, he edged toward the kitchen, then replaced the malfunctioning bug under the corner of the counter. This time, at least, the mutt didn't bark like hell. Daryl could handle a growl or two. He edged back toward the door. "That's right, Jasper, you little prick. I'm leaving now," he said, with an endearing tone. He inched open the door, slid outside, then twisted the lock, and gently pulled the handle until he heard the click.

He returned to his rental car, slipped inside, and started the engine, then set the GPS. With the radio turned down low, he settled in for the eight-hour drive and pondered how brilliantly his plan unfolded. Everything down to the most seemingly insignificant detail was set in place. For two years, he'd planned his revenge. At first, he researched every aspect of his mark's life. Slowly, he learned and absorbed everything he could about childhood, schooling, family, and friends.

Over time, he expanded his knowledge to encompass habits, dreams, and personal relationships. By the end of the first year, he'd saved enough money from his cross-country, eighteen-wheeler deliveries to buy state-of-the-art surveillance equipment and educated himself on how to use it. Once all the bugs were in place, he listened to intimate daily life, while he gathered background on "the others."

It sickened him to see what a privileged life his mark had lived—how spoiled and pampered. Daryl deserved that kind of upbringing. Instead, his momma scrimped and saved just to put food on the table. Her holier-than-thou, self-righteous parents disowned her when she told them she was pregnant.

She didn't disgrace her family. She worked her ass off to get through medical school. They should have been proud. And they should have believed her. Instead, they called her a slut. Said she lied when she claimed she was gang-raped by a bunch of drunken jocks at a graduation party.

She couldn't control what happened that night, and she didn't plan to get pregnant. But she sure as hell controlled whether or not to keep her own kid. If Daryl ever found out who his grandparents were, he'd make them pay, too.

Chapter Five

Arriving home at one o'clock a.m., Elise fell into bed fully dressed, until Jasper rambunctiously reminded her to take him outside. He bounded on top of her and licked her ear.

"Okay, boy. You win." Yawning, she trudged to the closet for his leash and attached it to his collar. When she opened the door, he shot outside, dragging her behind. She followed as Jasper took *her* for a walk in the park. Too tired to drag him back to the condo to lock the backdoor, she kept an eye on the porch.

A flashing blue light stabbing through the night sky immediately drew her attention and she stared beyond the park trees to the rear of the complex. She yanked on Jasper's leash to shorten the lead. "I see it, too, boy." She drew him closer. "I wonder what's going on."

"The police are knocking on all the doors in that section.

Pulse racing, she snapped around. In the dimly lit park, she didn't see the man approach. "Oh, God. You scared me to death."

"Sorry. I didn't mean to. I'm Jason Mallory."

"Nice to meet you, Jason. Do you frequently lurk in the park and sneak up on women after midnight?" She continued her stride toward the flashing lights.

"No." He chuckled and paced alongside. "I've been watching since the police arrived about twenty minutes ago. I live right over there." He pointed to a section of the development adjacent to the pool. "I've seen you around. You must live close."

"Yeah, I do." Since she lived in a gated community, it stood to reason they both lived close, but Elise wasn't in the habit of conversing with strangers.

As if sensing her caution, Jasper growled.

She was glad she had him next to her. Although, she expected the most he would do if confronted was lick the man to death. Still, Jason didn't know that, and she felt uncomfortable telling a complete stranger where she lived. She flashed him a glance, then shifting her gaze toward the police cars. She craned her neck to see the activity and edged closer. "So, what's going on over there?"

"The lady in 6B..." He paused a long beat before continuing. "Do you know her?"

Elise squinted as they approached the ambulance. "No. Is she sick or injured?"

"Neither. Not anymore." He shook his head. "From what I heard, the police received several calls from her friend. He was to pick her up for a dinner date. Her car was parked in the lot, but she didn't answer the door or her phone. He begged the police to check on her. They finally did. When she didn't answer the doorbell or a series of hard knocks, they broke in and found the poor woman––dead. Bruises around her neck indicated strangulation."

Elise's skin crawled, and she shivered. "Oh, my God. That's awful. The Enclave is gated and presumably a safe neighborhood."

His lips flattened, and he shrugged.

"That's why I chose this community."

"I hear ya." He stepped closer to the unravelling police scene.

Heart pounding, Elise felt a battle churn inside. She wanted to know more but discovering someone had been murdered just behind her condo twisted a knot in her stomach. As much as she loved covering the sports news, she didn't have the guts to cover violent crime. "I wonder if the murder was random—like a burglary gone bad—or someone she knew?"

Again, Jason shrugged. "I don't know the details. When neighbors began to line the street, we were pushed back, and the police told everyone to go home. I was curious, so I just walked back here to the park area."

"Well, I think going home is a good idea. If a woman was murdered, the killer could still be in the neighborhood. Thanks for letting me know,

Jason. Come on, boy." She turned and tugged Jasper's leash. "Let's go home."

"Nice to meet you," he called after her. "Maybe I'll see you around."

Elise didn't respond. Instead, she picked up her pace and rushed toward her building, then purposely walked around to the front door. She didn't know Jason Mallory. For all she knew, he could be the killer, and she didn't want him to know which condo was hers.

She reached behind a bush and under a rock for her emergency key. Turning the knob, she pushed open the door with her foot and stepped inside. She shut the door and flattened her back against the entrance. Even through her jacket, the gooseflesh on her arms prickled, and she drew in a long breath to relax her nerves.

Biting her lower lip, she wondered why dark stories and violence disturbed her so much. She hated horror movies and turned off newscasts covering local crime. Had she blocked a frightening event in her past? Or was she just a scared little girl at heart? She didn't know. But she couldn't shake the eerie chills violent scenes triggered.

After turning the deadbolt to double-lock the front door, she latched the back entry, as well, then unhooked Jasper's leash. As a rule, she never slept with her dog. She didn't even allow him on her bed. But tonight, a poor woman was murdered only a football field away, and she had no idea why. With a killer on the loose in her own backyard, Elise left on the closet light and cuddled with Jasper under the covers. Maybe, with him nestled next to her, she'd get some sleep. With little conviction, she closed her eyes.

Four thirty a.m. Saturday morning arrived far too fast. During basketball season, weekends meant a packed schedule. She showered and dressed, then took Jasper for a quick walk before heading to the office, stopping only briefly to go through the Starbucks drive-through. Venti latte in hand, she slid into a seat just as the morning's production meeting began.

When the meeting ended, she gathered her schedule, notes, and the day's headlines, and took them to her office where she sifted through and fleshed out the most gripping sports stories and organized her day. By eight o'clock, she was sitting in a cubical while her makeup artist did her magic with Elise's hair and face. Afterward, she checked in with her cameraman. By nine, she and Lance had their van packed and ready. They compared notes as they pulled out of the studio parking lot and headed toward their first stop. Today, they would interview Georgia Tech's head coach for a segment that would be aired on the six-p.m. news.

The pre-game show started at eleven a.m. Fortunately, Elise's schedule kept her too busy to think about the Enclave murder the night before or Deke's return to Atlanta.

The eight-hour drive flew by for Daryl. With only his thoughts for company, his strategy energized him, feeding a constant, slow-release stream of adrenaline to fuel his agenda. He hated altering any detail. Murdering that nosey neighbor across the park area wasn't planned. He didn't mean to kill her. His thoughts spun to what preceded the murder. When the old lady next door to Elise rattled the front doorknob, then slid a key into the lock, Daryl had little time to think. He barely escaped through the rear entrance.

If that hot young woman had only turned the other direction to walk her dog, she'd still be alive. But no. She saw Daryl slip out of Elise's condo, stared directly into his eyes, then she picked up her little dog and rushed home. No doubt she could identify him, and if she did, his entire plan would explode before the scheme even began. He couldn't let that happen or all his hard work would be for nothing. He didn't want to hurt the woman, especially a looker like her. But he had to eliminate the threat.

He followed her home, jimmied the lock, and crept inside through the backdoor before she came through the front. The woman never saw him coming. She bent over and detached the dog's leash from his collar. As she stood, Daryl's hand slid around her neck and covered her mouth.

The little dog viciously barked. Daryl shot a swift kick that sent the animal scurrying away.

"Don't...fight...me. I know you saw me sneaking out of that condo, but—"

She twisted, wriggling against him.

"I was just leaving her a rose——"

Struggling to escape his grip, she freed an arm and grabbed a vase from the foyer table, then shattered the glass behind his ear.

Daryl jerked her head against his chest and stared into her pleading eyes. In a brief moment, he watched her fear turn to terror, and then acceptance, as if she knew she was about to die. Twisting her around to face him, he heard a sharp crack. She went limp in his embrace, and a shot of heat sizzled through his arms and legs. He released his grip and glared at the terrified stare frozen on her face—a stare now etched into his mind. And every time he gazed into a mirror for the rest of his life, he'd see a cold-blooded killer.

His thoughts spun to his momma. She was the only woman who ever really loved him. What would she think of him now? He wished she mentioned her parents' names when she told him the truth on her deathbed. But she feared he'd avenge her, so, she never revealed their identity, and she was right. If she'd had the money to fight her cancer, she might have survived. Instead, he had to watch her slowly fade away to only a frail shadow of the woman who raised him. She suffered with excruciating pain, and Daryl felt powerless to do anything to help.

As much as he loved his momma, she was weak. She should have told the cops what happened. Had the filthy bastards arrested and thrown in jail for raping her. Instead, she ran away. Left her entire life behind. She changed her name and created a new life with her son. For that, Daryl was thankful. Still, she graduated with honors and could have had a lucrative career as a doctor. But under her new name, she could claim no diploma or papers to prove her education, so she settled for menial jobs.

Daryl bit off the tip of his fingernail, then spat to the side. He checked the rearview mirror, railing over his situation. He could have had a chance for an impressive career, too. A doctor's salary would pay the way for whatever he wanted. He might have been a doctor, a lawyer, an architect, an athlete, or a sportscaster. Instead, he drove a heavy rig cross country. Sure, the job paid good. And he was damn lucky to have such a solid occupation. But he'd never know what he might have achieved had he been given more options.

Fury seethed inside Daryl's veins. The bastards who raped his momma would pay for what they did. He'd track them down, every one of them, once he figured out who the hell they were. For now, he'd take on the devil he knew.

Daryl pulled into a spot on The Crown Plaza parking deck and turned off his rental car. Tired from the drive, he rode the elevator to the lobby and strolled into Taggart's for a good dinner. Sitting at a small table by the window, he gazed at the menu. Tonight, he would splurge.

"Good evening, sir. Would you care for a cocktail before dinner?"

"Whiskey. Straight up."

"Would you like top shelf or the house?"

"The house is fine."

"Yes, sir." The waiter pivoted and paced toward the bar.

Daryl leaned back into the plush chair. "Now, this is the life." He perused the menu.

When the waiter returned, he placed a napkin in front of Daryl, then a small glass of whiskey. "Would you care for an appetizer or are you ready to order?"

Daryl smiled. "I'll have your twelve-ounce sirloin steak topped with the chef's house-made made compound butter, a house salad with blue cheese dressing, au gratin potatoes, and asparagus."

"Yes, sir." Again, he turned. This time, he headed toward the kitchen.

Staring at the amber liquid, Daryl's thoughts spun. After two years of preparation, he would finally exact his revenge tomorrow, and this plan was   flawless.

Chapter Six

Gazing at his watch, Deke hustled through the airport toward the gate. The plane would board soon, and he wanted to grab a snack and drink to take on the flight. Seeing a McDonald's, he stepped to the shortest line and scanned at the menu. Why, he didn't know. He always ordered the same meal—a quarter pounder with cheese, a large fries, and a Coke. When his order came, he stuffed the sack into his duffle. Soft drink in hand, he flung his baggage over his left shoulder and rushed for the gate, arriving just as the passengers began boarding.

He lowered his bags and withdrew his ticket from the inside of his jacket, then weaseled his way through the crowd. When the staff called for first-class passengers, Deke shoved his way to the front of the line. After his boarding pass was scanned, he scooted down the ramp to the plane. Finding his seat, he rested his bags on the chair, placed his drink in the cupholder and retrieved his food. He took off his jacket and stuffed it next to his bags in the overhead area, then closed the compartment and slipped into his window seat. Drawing in a deep breath, he held the air for a long beat, then whooshed it out.

Once he was seated, the flight attendant leaned close.

"Can I bring you a drink, sir?" She smiled.

Deke considered the request, noting the late hour. He'd had a rough week. One drink would relax him. "Sure. Bring me a whiskey, please. No ice."

"You've got it." Nodding, she turned and disappeared behind the galley partition.

Threading his fingers behind his neck, Deke leaned against his hands. As an NFL player, he'd be traveling a lot more, and great salary aside, he looked forward to the perks.

The plane took off on time and was scheduled to land in Atlanta at ten p.m. He threw back the rest of his whiskey and peered out the window into the night sky.

His thoughts drifting to Elise, he dumped his food from the bag and laid it out on his tray. Smiling, he recalled yesterday's conversation with her. She said she couldn't wait to see him. But she had no idea how anxious he was to see her.

Elise woke up with a jolt from an erotic dream, her hair stringy and damp. Not because Deke fulfilled her wildest fantasies so vividly her entire body rippled with delight, but because as he kissed a path down her neck to her stomach, she opened her eyes to see a faceless man hovering over her, a knife gripped tightly in his left hand, poised to kill. She screamed as loud as she could, but no shriek burst through the silence. Deke faded into the distance, and she thrashed back and forth until she finally awoke in a cold sweat.

Jasper licked the moisture from her face, replacing it with his slippery slobber. Instead of pushing him away, she hugged him tightly, then reached for the dim lamp on her side table. Damn. Why did violent acts stick in her mind, spin through her dreams, and torment her like this? Her parents assured her she'd grow out of the scary nightmares. But they still clung to the corners of her mind and surfaced whenever she came in contact with disturbing incidents.

After a quick gaze at the clock, she gave Jasper a hug, then stood and trudged into the bathroom. Peering sideways in the mirror, she frowned and turned on the shower. Most Sundays, she'd be awake by now and on her way to work. But she took a vacation day to spend time with Deke. At least, his role in her nightmare was dream worthy. The thought of him kissing her entire body sent hot chills down her neck and shoulders, then spun down her arms and legs. She couldn't wait to see him.

When the water warmed, she stepped into the stall and let the stream envelop her. The hot spray somehow cleansed her from the eerie feeling that crushed her dream. She closed her eyes and thought about past moments with Deke. She'd never believed in love at first sight before she met him, but their first kiss changed her mind. Energized by excitement, she squirted a glob of body-wash into her mesh loofah, then squeezed it into a rich lather and scrubbed her body. After washing her hair, she rinsed off and lingered in the spray, relishing the feeling. Oh, what she'd give to be standing under the warm water with Deke. Envisioning the scene sent a visceral shot of heat between her thighs. When the water began to cool, she reluctantly stepped from the stall and grabbed a towel to dry off.

From the corner window, she saw the first rays of light breach the darkness. She slipped into her lounging pants and t-shirt, then blow-dried her hair. When most of the moisture was gone, she padded to the kitchen, made a cup of coffee, then hooked Jasper to his leash and took him outside.

She couldn't help but gaze across the park area to the condos beyond. Morbid curiosity coaxed her to peer at accidents and watch crime scenes unfold, but she couldn't shake the unnerving sensations that lingered weeks later. Perhaps, if she faced her fears, her anxiety would lessen. She rubbed the goosebumps prickling down her arms. "Come on, Jaz. Let's get you some breakfast." She tugged his leash and wandered inside.

By eleven fifteen, Elise was dressed and ready for her date with Deke. Gazing in the mirror, she touched up her blush and was brushing on lip gloss when the doorbell rang. A swirl of excitement rushed over her as she opened the front door. "I'm so glad you're home, Deke. I can't wait to hear everything about the Combine and your workouts." She smiled, then threw her arms around his neck and hugged him. "Come in."

He stepped inside and closed the door behind him, then scooped her into his arms and kissed her long and hard.

Lost in the release of pent-up passion, Elise fell limp.

When he finally stepped back, he smiled. "I've wanted that kiss for a long time." He gazed at her from foot to head. "You're breathtaking, Elise."

"Wow." Still quivering, she grinned.

He raised a brow and chuckled. "Sorry, I didn't mean to be so aggressive."

"The kiss was great. You've just never been quite so passionate before. But I'm glad you missed me." A pang of concern prickled down her arms. "Where's Jasper?" She tilted her head and gazed into the yard. "He didn't slip by us when we were distracted, did he?"

Deke scanned the room. "There he is, peering around the kitchen counter. I must have startled him, too. Come here, boy. I have a surprise for you."

Jasper stared and didn't move an inch until Deke drew a dog treat from his pocket and held it out.

"Sorry I scared you, boy. Here. Come get your treat."

Slowly, Jasper approached, then took the treat from Deke's hand and gobbled it down.

"Good boy." Deke turned toward Elise. "Damn. You're gorgeous. Are you ready to go to Ray's?"

"Absolutely. And I want all the details about the Combine. I'm so excited for you, Deke. You've worked so hard." She grabbed her coat from the closet.

"Let me help you." He held the wrap until she slid her arms inside the sleeves, then draped it over her shoulders. Opening the door, he shot a gaze toward Jasper. "We'll be back soon, buddy." He paused until Elise walked through the door, then slipped outside. Taking her hand, he headed toward his car and began his play-by-play diatribe about the entire week in Indianapolis.

Located on the Chattahoochee River on Powers Ferry Road, Ray's On The River was one of Elise's favorite restaurants, especially in the spring and summer when they could stroll the serene, landscaped grounds before and after a wonderful meal. But, even in late February, the view was beautiful, the food was five star, and the brunch was among the top one hundred in America. With prime-cut steaks, fresh seafood flown in daily, and regionally grown fruits and vegetables, the buffet was a masterpiece for any connoisseur.

Deke had made reservations for a corner table overlooking the river. The romantic setting made the entire experience perfect. Elise should have been over the moon, but she couldn't shake the unsettling anxiety churning inside.

The murder of that woman affected her more than she could explain away. "I can't fathom why anyone would murder someone like that."

Deke leaned forward and took her hand. "Who knows what awful demons lurk in the minds of people? I doubt the murder was random. Usually, a killer's actions are provoked by something."

She breathed in a gulp of air, then whooshed it out. "I know you're right." A chill twisted around her spine, sending a shiver down to her toes. She brushed her palms over her upper arms. "But I just can't shake this weird feeling of impending doom."

Chapter Seven

A week had passed since Deke returned home, and Elise still couldn't overcome her anxiety. Work provided a distraction, but she couldn't relax at night. By Sunday afternoon, she felt so anxious, she had to talk with someone aside from Deke.

After considering a professional, Elise called Britt, hoping to get a more insightful perspective. In a two-minute phone call, her friend had Elise feeling more relaxed than she'd felt the entire week. Britt suggested they meet at Cochran Shoals Trail for a walk and Elise agreed. Physical activity always reduced her angst, and she really missed hanging out with Britt. When the call ended, Elise breathed a sigh of relief. A hike along the Chattahoochee River would do wonders for both of them.

When Elise pulled into the parking area, she saw Britt leaning against her car, legs crossed and holding two water bottles. Britt knew her better than anyone in the world. She even anticipated

Elise would forget water. Smiling, she waved and parked the car.

When they started walking, Britt didn't waste a minute. "So, spill. What's going on?"

Elise pressed her lips together and shook her head. "I don't know. I just can't shake the creepy, eerie feeling I've had off and on all week."

Britt frowned. "Well, first of all, stop thinking something's wrong with you. Scary shit has given you the heebie-jeebies for as long as I've known you. And a murder so close would make anyone a bit on edge—even me."

"After what you do for a living, I doubt that. But thanks." Elise gazed at the river rushing around a fallen tree. "I feel better just getting outside like this."

"I'm glad. But I'm not kidding, Elise. I'd be nervous, too. What concerns me more is how you've felt around Deke. He's the catch of a lifetime, girl. For months you've practically felt like he could walk on water. Are you having second thoughts?"

"No...maybe...I mean, I'm sure it's just anxiety. I'm oversensitive because of the murder." A dog barked in the distance, and she flashed on Jasper's hesitance to take the treat Deke offered.

Britt tightened her ponytail. "Okay, so, how does Deke fit into that? How has he made you feel?"

Elise watched a squirrel chase another around a tree, then jump branch to branch. "I feel like that squirrel being chased." She turned toward Britt and acknowledged her blank stare. "I know. That makes no sense. And I'm sure my edgy feelings have nothing to do with him. I love Deke with all my heart but, since the murder, little things get on my nerves."

"Like what?" Britt frowned.

An animal rustled through the leaves and Elise gasped. Her gaze snapped to the underbrush.

Britt raised her brows toward her forehead. "Like that?"

"Probably. I haven't slept well, and I know I'm jittery, but things I never noticed Deke did before agitate me—like interrupting me mid-sentence, micro-managing how I do things, and he constantly fondles me."

"I wouldn't mind that last one." Britt chuckled.

Elise pursed her lips. "I know, but at weird, inappropriate times, like I'm his possession and he can slip his hand over any part of my body whenever he wants. Have you ever seen him do that?"

"Honestly, no." She squeezed her eyebrows together. "Deke has nothing but the utmost respect for you. In fact, he's really respectful of women in general."

Turning onto the wooden bridge, Elise stopped and gazed at the river. "I know. You're right. It's just me." She shot a gaze toward Britt. "So why now? When everything in my life is so good? The last thing I want is to blow up my relationship with Deke." The cool air above the water bit at her cheeks. To block the breeze, she spun and leaned against the railing.

Britt tugged Elise's arm and started walking the path again. "I'm not an analyst, but——"

Elise broke in. "Do you think I need one?"

"No. I mean, nothing's wrong with seeing a doctor. But think about this. Deke just completed probably the toughest, most stressful week of his life, and you've been working a crazy schedule—not to mention the man of your dreams just proposed a few weeks ago. Throw in a murder so close to home? Both of you have been super stressed. You need a break."

Nodding, Elise agreed. "Maybe we should get away for a few days and just relax."

"We talked about you taking him to your family's cabin at Lake Lanier. You could hike to the waterfalls, sit by the firepit at night, make love in the hot tub. Do it, Elise. A relaxing, romantic holiday is just what you both need."

"You're right." As she envisioned the scene, the tension in her neck and shoulders relaxed.

"Of course, I am." Britt chortled.

"What a perfect idea. This week is his spring break, and the weather is still cool enough to do all those things. I'm sure I could take a few days off since I've been volunteering for so many games lately." She halted, then hugged Britt. "You're a genius."

"So people say. Ha, I never get tired of hearing how brilliant I am."

Elise gave her a shove. "Seriously, I feel so much better. Thanks for suggesting we take a walk here. I really love this trail. The water relaxes me."

"It doesn't take a genius to know walking is a great way to de-stress. I'm glad I could help. You've straightened out my butt enough times. We make a good tag team."

They continued their walk around the 5k loop, taking in the stunning scenes of the Chattahoochee River and exploring the marshes and woods along the trail. The afternoon re-energized Elise and gave her the new perspective she needed to get past her angst.

When the sun sank low in the sky, Elise gave Britt a hug, then returned to her car and drove home, excited to make plans with Deke. She pulled into the lot and parked in her spot, then flung her purse over her shoulder and paced toward her condo.

"Hey, pretty lady."

Elise spun toward the voice to see Jason Mallory approaching. She feigned a smile.

"Did you hear any more about the lady in six-B?"

"No. But I've been pretty busy. You?"

"Only that the police ruled out family and friends." He leaned against the split rail post and crossed one shoe over the other. "Since nothing appeared to be missing, they doubt she walked in on a burglar."

Elise frowned. The thought of a killer randomly roaming her condo complex tightened her throat. She swallowed hard. "Then who killed her? Do they have any suspects?"

"Not yet, at least, they aren't making public whatever they know."

She gazed at the ground and kicked at a pebble on the curb. "Hmm. I can't imagine the incident was a random attack." Raising her gaze, she observed Jason. He was tall, blond, with grey eyes, a mustache, and a short-cropped beard. The night she met him, she couldn't see his face as well as she could now, in broad daylight. He looked like a nice-enough man. Not her vision of the Boston Strangler. "Do you know where the woman worked?"

"I have no idea." He shrugged. "But now that you mention it, I wonder if a colleague might have held some kind of a grudge."

"Or a competitor. With all the DNA and high-tech advances, I have no doubt they'll nail the killer. Thanks for the update. Nice seeing you, Jason." She turned and strolled toward her condo.

"You, too," Jason replied. "See you later."

Elise breathed a sigh of relief. The walk and talk had improved her state of mind, and the possibility the murder wasn't random calmed her nerves even more. When she reached her porch, she saw a single white rose in a vase next to her door. She reached for the card and read: *I hope your walk with Britt helped you relax. I love you. Deke.*

She pressed the note against her chest and smiled. Pushing open the door, she grabbed the vase and stepped inside. As she set her purse on the foyer table, Jasper bounded toward her with his typical, excited greeting. She placed the bud on the kitchen counter, then leaned over to pet her pup. "Okay, boy. I'm happy to see you, too."

He nosed open the closet door and tugged on his leash until it slipped from the hook, then he brought it to Elise.

She chuckled. "I guess that means you want to go for a walk." She attached the leash to his collar then, opening the back door, she gazed at the beautiful white rose. Her stomach suddenly clenched. She hadn't spoken to Deke since she phoned Britt. How did he know where she was today?

Chapter Eight

The knot in her stomach twisted. *Relax, Elise. Don't be so paranoid.* A logical explanation for Deke's note must exist.

"Oh, hello, dear." Mrs. Murphy smiled. "And you, too, Jasper." She returned her gaze to Elise. "When my dear Brandi passed, I wanted to get another Yorkie, but my son convinced me not to. His wife doesn't like dogs and won't have one in their home...especially now that the twins arrived. A dog would make traveling more difficult, too. I don't see how you manage, dear, but I'm glad I can help." She puffed the pillows on her porch swing.

"Thank you, Mrs. Murphy. Jasper loves you, too, and I appreciate you watching him when I have to go on road trips."

I don't mind at all." She gave Jasper a scrunch. "Your boyfriend, Deke, is a real charmer. I ran into him when he brought you the rose. Any man who brings a woman flowers for no reason is a keeper." Grabbing a feather duster, she busily dusted the table and chair adjacent to the swing.

"Yes...he's a keeper." Ah, that's how Deke knew Britt and Elise hiked Cochran Shoals. She'd seen Mrs. Murphy earlier, sweeping her deck, and asked her to keep an ear out for Jasper. "When you saw Deke, did you mention where I was?"

She paused her dusting and frowned. "He rang the doorbell several times to give you the rose. I didn't think you'd mind."

"Oh, you're fine, Mrs. Murphy. I don't mind at all. I just wondered how he knew." The knot in her stomach relaxed. Why did she doubt him? Britt was right. Deke was the man of her dreams. Elise needed to stop thinking about the incident across the park and focus on her own life.

"Whew. I'm glad, dear. He's such a sweet and thoughtful boy."

"I need to get this one to the park." Elise hitched her head toward Jasper. "He's been cooped up "Of course, dear. Run along."

"See you later." Elise tugged on Jasper's leash and dug into her pocket for her phone. Strolling toward the grassy area, she pressed the side button. "Call Deke."

"Calling Deke," the voice command replied.

When he answered the line, she gushed, "So, Mrs. Murphy says you're a keeper."

"She does? And what do you say?"

A smile tugged at the corners of her mouth. "I think she's a smart woman." Elise gazed across the park at a lingering crime scene ribbon fluttering in the breeze and purposely turned away. "The rose is beautiful, Deke. Thanks."

"You're welcome. I just wanted you to know I was thinking about you."

Convinced a weekend away with Deke would calm her nerves, she brought up the idea. "I have a surprise for you, too. Well, not really a surprise. More of an outing. We've both had a grueling schedule lately, and I could really use a break. Do you think you could ditch everything this weekend and go to the lake house?"

The long silence ensuing caught her off guard. He loved going to the lake. "If you can't get away, it's fine. We don't have to do it this weekend." She held her breath, waiting for his reply.

"Sorry. I was just visualizing my calendar, preparing for the Combine dominated my life for months, but now that it's over. Sure. A weekend getaway with you. I'm in."

She whooshed the breath from her lungs. "Great. We can make plans later."

"Sounds good. I've got some studying to do tonight so I'll talk to you tomorrow."

"Thanks again for the rose. I love it." When they first started dating, Elise thought Deke was just a charmer. But over time, she realized what a thoughtful man he was, randomly giving her little gifts for no apparent reason. She tucked a stray clump of hair behind her ear. "Most men buy flowers for special occasions, but you never need a reason. I love that."

"How do you know?"

"How do I know what?"

He chuckled. "That I don't have an ulterior motive?"

"I don't." Again, the hairs on the back of her neck prickled.

Kicking at the dirt along the trail, Daryl cussed. Now that Elise decided to come to the lake for the weekend, he'd have to move his rig and cover any tire prints that might indicate an eighteen-wheeler had parked on the long stretch of gravel road that led to the cabin. Why did his scheme run into so many unexpected roadblocks? He'd planned out everything so carefully...down to each detail. He even anticipated various scenarios and created backup plans for each one. But he couldn't get inside Elise Sloan's head. Why did she have to bring Deke to the lake house this weekend?

Stomping over the uneven gravel, he stumbled, his ankle rolling. He bent over and rubbed the injury until the pain subsided, then he snatched the offending rock and lobbed it across the smooth water. *Wait a minute.* He observed the landscape, scanning a three-hundred-sixty-five-degree circumference around where he stood. He saw no one. He heard nothing but squirrels rustling through the underbrush and an occasional bird chirp. In the distance, he picked up the faint hum of an outboard motor. Across the lake, he saw no signs of development. No people, homes, or beaches. Only miles of dense woods lined the shore. The silent cove bore no waves. Not even the slightest current. The sun reflected off the glass-like surface and sparkled with glints of gold that glittered against a crystal glass surface.

He tramped through the forest in search of a level area close enough to the Sloans' cabin to be accessible but a sufficient distance to keep curious hikers from seeing his rig. With the lake to his left, he could easily find his way back to the cabin.

This land wasn't simply a family cabin on Lake Lanier, it was a huge track of private property. He could park as deep in the woods as his cab could drive and hide from the world. How had he missed this? The revelation he initially tagged as a pain in the ass, he now realized gave him an incredible advantage. Elise's sudden desire for a weekend getaway to her family cottage dropped in Daryl's lap the perfect setup. He grinned so big his cheeks hurt as everything fell into place.

Finally, he would have the life he dreamed of. But it didn't come easily. He thought about how hard he'd worked to get here...how he scrimped and saved to earn enough money to finance his revenge. Driving his rig across country for years gave him a lot of time to think, and plan.

Circling back to the gravel road, he thought about his momma. When she died, she left him everything, which wasn't much. But Daryl knew patience and diligence would reap rewards. He leased the house, and the money he got from the rent paid his own rental fees for a semi-truck. Who knew he'd get paid seventy thousand dollars a year to simply drive? Ha.

He did his homework…and pocketed his pay. He did his homework and pocketed his pay. When he finally saved enough to buy his own rig, he bought a good-sized sleeper, then built it out to his own specifications, with every basic creature comfort. A bed, shower, toilet, fridge, everything a captive could want—except windows. A single, steel door, padlocked from the driver's seat, would ensure his personal guests stayed put. Cameras and a two-inch sliding rectangular opening for emergency access. He added soundproofing, too, to make sure no one heard a random cry for help.

By the time he returned to his truck, he had a real sense of the cabin's location and the surrounding area and had found the perfect parking spot. He hopped into the driver's seat and switched the ignition, then veered off the gravel where the wheels would be least likely to leave tracks and maneuvered his way through the woods. Grabbing a toothpick from the ashtray, he slid it between his teeth and pondered how diligent he'd been since Momma died.

He learned investigative skills and surveillance methods over the Internet he accessed at truck stops, and he worked out every day. When he drove his loads, he listened in on his mark. Driven by revenge, he never lacked motivation. His momma would be proud how determined and focused he was, always keeping his eye on the prize. He was close. So close he could taste victory, and it was so sweet.

Chapter Nine

The week flew by. Monday through Thursday, Elise awoke every day at four thirty a.m. and went through her typical schedule, then, on top of her regular load, she covered extra games so she could take off Friday through Monday for a long weekend. With little time to worry and no time to see Deke, her excitement about the getaway built exponentially each day.

She knew, with final exams fast approaching, Deke was relieved to have extra time to study. He'd planned to hunker down over Spring Break, but no way he'd miss going to Elise's lake house. So, to make up the study time, he promised to play catch-up with his tutor this week, instead. He'd have to cram to be fully prepared by May fifth. Football and the Combine took a lot of time away from his classes and the last thing he wanted was to flunk out the last Thursday night, Elise dragged during the last game, and when she finally got home, she fell into bed fully clothed and completely exhausted. But excitement for the weekend getaway awakened her fifteen minutes before her alarm rang. She popped out of bed and gave Jasper his morning dose of attention, then went to her closet to choose her attire for the day. Convinced this weekend would do wonders for her relationship with Deke, she mentally planned every detail she could think of to create a perfectly romantic getaway. She wanted so badly to feel the chemistry they shared for the last six months—the chemistry that somehow had faded over the last few weeks.

She threw on a pair of jeans and a sweatshirt, then strolled into the kitchen. After pouring a cup of coffee, she peered through the window, sipping the hot brew. A cold nose nudging her free hand told her Jasper wanted to go outside.

Shifting her gaze, she smiled at Jaz, leash hanging from his mouth and tail wagging.

"Good boy." She patted his head. "Let's make our walk quick today. I've got a lot to do before we go to the lake." She attached his lead and flipped up the catch so he could have more rope, then opened the back door. Before she could give him the okay, he shot outside. "Whoa, slow down, buddy."

He immediately stopped and sniffed the greenery.

A crisp breeze rushed through her still-damp hair, prompting chills to ripple down her arms. She gazed across the park to the condos beyond, then turned away, intentionally changing her thoughts to a more productive focus. She scrolled her phone to her daily to-do notes and added items to the grocery list. Ribeye steaks, fresh Brussels sprouts to sprouts to slice and roast, baked potatoes with butter, chives, sour cream, and bacon—all Deke's favorites—plus a nice red wine. She'd ask someone at the little wine shop for a recommendation.

The cabin stocked all the condiments and accessories she'd need so she didn't have to buy steak sauce, wine glasses, or a nice tablecloth, but she wanted to find a pretty centerpiece for the table. Since her parents retired and moved to Florida, they only visited the lake during the heat of the summer. Now, the house was virtually Elise's any time she wanted.

She loved the place and would live there permanently if it wasn't so far from work. As it was, she spent as much time there as she could. She knew the lay of the land, all the best beaches and private coves, and even a secret waterfall with a giant rock perfect for picnics. The weather report predicted an unseasonably warm weekend, and she hoped Deke would be up for a hike.

When his face suddenly appeared on her screen, Elise smiled. "Hey, babe. I'm surprised to hear from you so early. What's up?"

"Hey, beautiful. I just wanted to let you know coach has a senior meeting at one o'clock this afternoon. I know you wanted to leave for the lake by ten, but no can do."

"Oh, Deke. What time can you leave?"

"I hope by two, but don't wait. You go ahead and take Jasper. I'll meet you there as soon as I can get away."

"That works. I have some shopping to do for dinner and, arriving early will give me time to change the bedsheets and make sure we have everything we need before you get there."

"Perfect. I can't wait. I'm really looking forward to some alone time with you, away from the real world."

"Me, too. Drive safely. And let me know if your meeting runs late."

"Will do. You be safe, too. I'll see you before you know it." He ended the call.

Elise sat on the park bench and extended Jasper's lead to full length. She stared across the park, her thoughts reeling. Of course, she wished Deke could spend the day with her at the lake, but maybe this arrangement was better. She hadn't been to the lake house for a few months. There was bound to be something she needed that she hadn't thought of. This way, she could take care of all the minutia she'd typically have to buy locally before Deke arrived. And if she didn't need to run to the store, she and Jasper could take a short hike along the shoreline.

A tug on the leash returned her attention to Jasper. She stood. "Come on, Jaz. Let's go home."

He raced toward her and let out a soft woof.

After packing her clothes and accessories, she gathered what she wanted to take for the weekend, including Jasper's food and bed, then piled everything into the backseat of the BMW.

"Jasper, do you want to go for a ride?"

Tail wagging, he bounced up and down on his front paws.

Elise grabbed his leash. "Let's go, buddy." She locked the condo door behind her.

Jasper shadowed her every step then, when she opened the car door, he jumped into the passenger seat.

After a quick stop at the local Kroger to buy the items on her grocery list, she was on her way to the lake. She set her radio to her favorite music station and headed north on Route 400. The trip was an easy drive and, passing the Avalon Mall and Bald Ridge Marina energized her. She'd spent so much time at the lake as a child, the cabin felt like home and the ambiance calmed her. Britt was right. This weekend getaway was exactly what she needed.

By the time Elise turned onto the long gravel road that led to her cabin, it was almost noon. Aside from drinking a cup of coffee, she didn't stop long enough to eat or drink anything since she woke. Thank goodness she'd anticipated ahead and packed sandwich fixings.

Still bare from the cold weather, the tall hardwoods lining the road looked callous, stark, and dismal. Not the lush green warmth that greeted her during spring, summer, and fall. The two-mile gravel road that usually instilled a calm excitement now flooded her with unnerving tension. She stiffened as the eerie sensation swept over her and shot a shiver down her neck that settled at the base of her spine. Turning up the radio, she pressed her foot on the accelerator and the tires spat gravel behind her. *Get a grip, Elise.*

She lifted her foot and pressed the brake until the car slowed to a crawl. The rush of anxiety dissipated. *What the hell was that?* Of all the places on Earth, the cabin and surrounding landscape had always soothed her frazzled nerves. Normally, she felt safe here. Peering through the windshield toward the sun, she took in the sparkling blue sky. Bright sunbeams glittered off the bare branches.

Jasper snuggled close and pressed his nose against her wrist.

She lowered her gaze. "It's okay, boy. I'm fine." Shaking off the gloom, she picked up her speed to a normal pace and set her mind, determined to calm the stress of the last few weeks. She drew in a long breath. The house was just around the bend, and she knew spending the weekend in her favorite hideaway would give her the rest and relaxation she sorely needed.

Chapter Ten

Pulling up to the house, Elise felt a sense of calm swathe her into total relaxation. She parked and opened the car door.

Immediately, Jasper bounded over her onto the soft fescue and dashed toward the fishpond to lap several drinks from the waterfall.

She smiled, watching him sniff and peer at the koi as they scattered, then he ran to the opposite side of the pond and repeated the game. Gazing around the estate, she stretched to release the kinks in her neck and shoulders and strolled toward Jasper, her mind conjuring memories.

For years, her father crafted every foot of the yard, landscaping the grounds with perennials and shrubs, interspersed with trails and a plush, carpet-like lawn. A beautiful, rocky stream ran through the property, twisting and turning as the water flowed over the stones, then cascaded into the koi pond. The footpath wrapped in and out of evergreen shrubs and was lined with assorted flowers that bloomed throughout the year.

Occasionally, the trail veered onto small footbridges across the water. The backyard, facing the lake, sported a stone firepit, hiding the pump that drew in lake water and spat it into the handcrafted stream. In every direction, Elise saw the love her dad poured into their property. "You love this place, too. Don't you, boy?"

Jasper woofed.

She leaned over and scratched his head. "Come on, Jaz. Let's go inside and get settled." After a quick gaze across the cove, she drew in a long breath and smiled. "Deke will be here before we know it and I want everything perfect." She turned toward the car.

Jasper trotted to the vehicle and jumped inside. Grasping hold of his bed, he tugged until it cleared the console. Then, he hauled the pad to the porch.

"How did you get so smart, boy?" Laughing at her exceedingly intelligent pup, Elise grabbed her purse and a load of groceries, then followed him to the porch. Gazing downward, she chuckled. "What? You can't open the door, too?"

He sat and lightly pawed her thigh.

She juggled her load and gave him a scratch behind his ear, then dug the key from her handbag and unlocked the front entrance.

Before she could completely shove open the door, he raised on his hind feet and pushed against the solid wood. The door flew open.

Elise shook her head and walked inside behind him. She dropped her load on the farmhouse table and gazed around the open great room. As much as she loved the grounds, the lake, and the woods beyond, she loved the cabin more. The structure took rustic to a whole new level, and though rough-sawn beams accented the interior walls, glass windows lined the entire rear of the house, making the deck and lake visible from every room.

After retrieving everything she brought, she put away the groceries, then strolled out back and checked the hot tub temperature. One hundred four degrees. Perfect. Like always, Mr. Bailey, the caretaker her father had watching the property, followed her directions to a tee.

"Alexa, play Elise's playlist." With her favorite music blaring in the background, she sang along, busily searching the linen closet for a tablecloth and napkins. She draped the table, set out plates, wine glasses, and utensils, then added a fat vanilla candle to her centerpiece. She checked the pantry to make sure she had all the condiments needed for dinner. Stepping outside, she fetched three logs, then crafted a teepee of wood in the great room fireplace and added kindling and tucked in a few crumpled newspaper sheets to ensure the flames would burn long enough to ignite the logs. When everything was set, she admired her handiwork, then went upstairs.

After unpacking her clothes, she put them away, then changed the bed linens. When she finished the chores, she glanced at her cell phone. No texts from Deke meant at least two hours before he'd arrive. Time enough to take Jasper on a hike along the beach. "Jaz, let's go for a walk."

Two seconds later, he was by her side.

She snatched the leash from the bar, then thought better of the idea and hung it by the door. The Sloan acreage ran for miles. Her gramps purchased the land for next to nothing before Lake Lanier was built. Eighty-seven acres of prime property, much of which was lakeside, would bring in a ton of money, even in the nineteen fifties. But Gramps only sold a small tract. He wanted the land for his family. No one lived even remotely close, and Elise never saw anyone while walking along the beach. "Let's go, buddy. You don't need a leash here."

The moment she opened the rear French doors, Jasper shot outside in front of her and galloped around the fire pit before returning. Then he paced alongside, keeping up with her every step as she strode across the plush backyard and turned onto the sandy beach.

She loved listening to the silence, which was, to her, predominantly the soft sounds of nature, a chipmunk rustling through the leaves, a squirrel chasing his mate around a tree trunk, then skittering from tree to tree on the branch highway. Birds chirping, the soft splash of tiny waves lapping against the shore, and the distant hum of a faraway boat motoring across the water. The lake silence always calmed her, and she was so thankful for her family refuge.

Picking up a random stick, she tossed it down the beach. "Go get it, Jaz."

The dog took off running, retrieved the stick, then raced back to Elise. The game continued over and over. He never tired of playing fetch.

When the weather was warmer, she would throw a stick into the lake, and Jaz would happily swim out, chomp hold of the twig, and return to Elise. But on her last throw, when she threw the wood, he ran toward it then stopped cold.

A moment later, he sped into the forest and out of sight.

Elise took off after him. "Jaz. Come here, boy." She whistled, but he didn't return. She heard him barking feverishly in the distance. "Jasper. Come. Now." But Jasper continued to bark deep within the woods.

When her cellphone beeped, she dug the device from her back pocket and glanced at the screen. She read Deke's text.

Meeting over. OMW. Should be at the house around 5.

Without replying, she stuffed the phone into her back pocket and continued toward the sound of Jasper's bark, pushing aside vines as she tramped through the thick woodland. "Jaz. Come here." Why wouldn't he respond to her command? He'd never ignored her before. A wave of adrenaline shot down her back as she lumbered deeper into the dense forest glen.

Chapter Eleven

Jasper sprang through the brush, startling Elise. She spun, and her hand flew to her chest. "Dear Lord, Jaz. You scared me to death." She leaned over to scrunch behind his ear. "Why did you run off like that, boy?" After taking several long breaths of relief, she yanked on his collar. "Let's go, buddy. We need to get back to the cabin."

Jasper lightly clamped his jaws around her wrist and tugged—his slobbery method of letting her know he wanted her to follow.

But his excursion would have to wait today. She pulled her arm from his grasp and knelt beside him. "No, Jaz. We can't hike through the woods right now. Deke will be at the cabin soon." She stood and again, pulled on his collar.

Instead of complying and following Elise, he chomped down on the hem of her jacket and pulled.

She wrinkled her brow, annoyed he hadn't acquiesced as he typically did. "I know you love to hike the forest, boy, but we can't do that now." She crooked a finger under his collar and tugged until he complied. "Good boy. I promise we'll hike tomorrow."

Once Elise broke through the woods and onto the beach, she jogged along the waterfront, hoping to tire Jasper more than exercise herself. But the run released pent-up energy that soothed her anxiety, and by the time she reached the cabin, she felt an endorphin rush that completely removed the edge and boosted her mood. She burst through the back door. "Alexa, play Elise's romantic mix." After removing her jacket, she hung it on a laundry room hook, then stripped off her sweaty clothes as she ran upstairs toward the shower.

The hot cascade felt so good, she stood under the rainwater longer than she planned, singing along with the romantic tunes playing in the background. When she finally dragged herself from the relaxing spray, she dried and styled her hair, then put on the perfect outfit for the evening—an off-the-shoulder, baby pink sweater over a black lace camisole, black high-waisted jeans, and her super cute, black ankle boots.

Makeup on and hair done, she floated down the stairs, still humming to the music. A glance at her watch told her Deke would arrive any moment. She grabbed the long-tipped lighter from the mantel and lit the kindling for the fire, then went into the kitchen to pour a glass of wine and start dinner.

Busily cooking, Elise didn't hear a knock on the front door or the bell, but Jasper's persistent barking alerted her someone was lurking around the yard. She stepped into the great room and gazed at him, still woofing at the door. "Jaz. It's Deke. Hush."

A sharp tap on the glass adjacent to the farmhouse table startled her, and she spun to see Deke, holding a bouquet of white roses.

Growling, Jasper sped toward the back door. Pressing his front paws against the glass, again, he let out a low snarl. "Rrrrrrrrrrrr."

Elise shook her head and shrugged. "It's okay, Jaz." She scooted past him and walked around the table to open the door.

But Deke turned the knob and walked in before she could.

He met her, placed the flowers on the table, and hugged her. "How was your day, babe?"

Again, Jasper growled. "Rrrrrrrrrr."

"What has gotten into you, boy? It's just Deke." She shifted her gaze to her doting fiancé. "Sorry about that."

"I think he's jealous I brought you a gift and I didn't bring him one." He dug into his pocket and pulled out a dog biscuit, then offered the treat to Jasper. "Here you go, Jaz. I didn't forget you, boy."

The dog tentatively stepped closer, then snatched the biscuit and retreated, leaping up the stairway to the hallway. From his favorite perch, he watched them through the banister rails and chomped on the treat.

Elise chuckled and shrugged. "He's acted strangely all day." Turning, she reached for the exterior alarm and flipped it on, a habit her parents taught to alert the family if someone turned onto their private driveway.

Deke drew in a long breath. "Hmmm. What smells so good in the kitchen?"

"Just the potatoes baking. I have ribeye steaks, though. Can you light the grill while I put the veggies into the oven?"

"Sure. Would you like me to do the grilling?"

"Absolutely." Elise walked to the fireplace, grasped the lighter then handed it to Deke.

He grabbed her wrist, then drew her close and kissed her.

When he stuck his hard tongue down her throat, she pulled away. "Let me get you a glass of wine."

He released her, then turned toward the door and gripped the knob.

She spun and walked into the kitchen, attempting to shake off his brashness. She much preferred the soft, sensual kisses that made her toes curl.

As Deke opened the deck door, he gazed over his shoulder. "How do you like your steak cooked?"

Elise peered around the corner and frowned. "The same way you always cook them."

"Right. Burnt, as usual." He stepped outside.

Gasping, Elise rushed to the door. "Don't you dare burn them. Medium-rare to medium."

He chuckled. "Just kidding."

She shook her head and ducked inside. After placing the prepared Brussels sprouts in the oven, she switched the dial to roast and set the timer, then sprinkled the steaks with Montreal Steak Seasoning. She poured a glass of wine for Deke, topped off hers, then carried them outside. "Here, I hope you like the wine. The sommelier highly recommended a Bordeaux to pair with steak. This one is a blend, full-bodied with notes of smoke, plum, black currant, and tobacco." She chuckled.

He took the glass and sniffed. "Nice bouquet." After taking a small sip, he swished the liquid, then swallowed. "Good choice. I think the sommelier was spot on."

She smiled. "The steaks are ready. Is the grill hot enough?"

"Not yet." He took a long swig of his wine and strolled toward the spa. "What do you say we sit in the hot tub after dinner?"

"I'd say that's exactly what I planned."

He scanned the backyard. "Damn. This property must have set your folks back a pretty penny. How much do you think this place is worth?"

She squinted...as if in doing so she might understand why he asked. "I told you my granddad bought this tract of land before the lake was built. Besides, it doesn't matter how much it's worth. My parents have already gifted the land to me, and I'll never sell the property. It's my home."

"I know, babe. I was just speculating." He returned to the grill. "Why don't you grab those steaks for me, hon?"

Elise turned and walked inside. Lately, every time she started to feel good about Deke, he blurted out something that rubbed her the wrong way. Not that his comment was awful, but it just felt odd. She checked the sprouts. Deke liked them brown and crispy, so she'd leave them in a bit longer.

She picked up the steaks and brought them to Deke then stared at the lake. The full moon reflecting off the water cast a glimmer across the surface that sparkled with the current. Taking another sip of wine, she shifted her gaze toward Deke. She loved him so much. Why couldn't she shake her angst? She couldn't wait to cuddle next to him by the fireside…or get passionate in the spa under the shimmering moonlight. She wanted so badly to have a perfect weekend.

"Steaks are ready, sweet pea. Let's chow down."

"I'll get the potatoes and veggies. Do you need more wine?"

"Absolutely."

She shot a gaze his way. Deke never drank more than one glass. But football was over, and the Combine behind him. Maybe having a few more drinks would relax both of them.

She slipped on an Ov-Glove and pulled the vegetables from the oven, then placed them on the table and sat.

Deke brought in the steaks and served one to Elise and put the other on his plate, then set the dish aside and sat next to her. "Great dinner, hon. Dig in." He cut a slice of steak and jammed it into his mouth. "Delicious, if I do say so myself, but it looks like you burnt the vegetables." His gaze narrowed. "What was that dish, anyway?"

Elise frowned. "Brussels sprouts."

"Not a fan. But I'll try anything once."

A knot fisted in her stomach. She lowered her fork and stared at Deke, then swallowed hard. Who was this man sitting next to her?

Chapter Twelve

Pinching together her eyebrows, Elise glared, remembering countless times Deke told her roasted Brussels sprouts were his favorite vegetable.

"Just kidding." Deke laughed. "Lighten up, babe." He clasped a hand over hers and softly squeezed. "Ever since the incident in your neighborhood, you've been jumpy and stressed. This weekend, we both need to relax and block out the rest of the world."

Uncomfortable with his apparent joke, she bit the corner of her lip. "You're right." Tucking a loose strand of hair behind her ear, she smiled. "I really want us to have a wonderful weekend...I don't know why that poor woman's murder has me so on edge." Elise took another sip of wine, then carved a bite of steak and slipped it into her mouth. The slice of perfectly grilled ribeye almost melted as the flavor swirled over her tongue. "Mmmm. Perfect. Kudos Chef Madigan. My steak is delicious."

The rest of the meal, they continued their small talk, primarily questions from Deke about Elise's week. He wanted a play-by-play of every game she covered. When he finished his steak and baked potato, he shoved the sprouts around the plate, then wiped his mouth with a napkin and pushed away from the table. "I have a great idea. Why don't we move over in front of the fire and have another glass of wine? I've had a rough week, and I really would like to sit back, put my feet up, and wrap my arms around you." He stood and patted his stomach. "Damn good meal, babe. By the way, did I tell you how beautiful you look tonight?"

"I think you mentioned it a couple of times, but I never get tired of hearing you tell me." She stood and began clearing the dishes. "I'll just throw these in the dishwasher and join you in a few minutes." She stared at the empty bottle of wine and shook her head. Having only brought one bottle to the lake house, she'd have to raid her dad's wine cellar to select another. Not that he'd mind her taking whatever she wanted, but she felt odd over Deke indulging in more than one alcoholic beverage.

Again, she reminded herself that Deke's brutal football schedule just ended, and they both needed to unwind. "Hey, babe, I have to run downstairs for another bottle of wine. Do you have a preference?"

Raising his brows, he tilted his head and ogled her from head to toe. "How about some champagne? I have a lot to celebrate."

His tone made her skin crawl, and his stare. She felt like he physically undressed her with his gaze. "I...I don't know what Dad has in his cellar, but I'll look for champagne." She opened the cellar door and stepped downstairs, rationalizing the eerie sensation triggered by his request. She wanted Deke to be attracted to her. Why did his sexual gaze tonight make her feel creepy?

Scanning the wine cooler for some bubbly, she spotted a Crémant de Loire sparkling Sancerre. She snatched the bottle. Maybe she was having second thoughts about marrying Deke. The love of her life. The man who made her toes curl the first time they kissed. No. She loved him. Her anxious thoughts had nothing to do with him.

She turned and marched up the steps, then closed the cellar door behind her. Determined to overcome her anxiety once and for all, she grabbed two flutes from the cabinet, then strolled into the great room and sat next to Deke. She handed him the wine and set the flutes on the table. "I think this Sancerre will do the trick."

Deke took the bottle and peeled off the foil. After popping the cork, he filled the flutes and handed one to Elise. He held up his glass and tipped it toward hers. "To us. May we have the life I've dreamed of."

Elise clinked his glass. "To us." She took a long sip, then set her wine on the coffee table and stared at the roaring fire.

After downing half of his drink, Deke set aside the flute, then twisted toward Elise. He wrapped his arms around her and drew her close. After pushing a chunk of hair behind her ear, he clutched his hand around the bulk of her mop, yanked back her head, and began kissing and licking around her ear. Nuzzling her hairline, he ran his moist, hot tongue and lips all over her neck and bare shoulder.

The yank surprised her, and for a moment, she stiffened, but when he kissed along her neck, she began to relax.

With his teeth, he tugged at her camisole until it fell down her arm. He slid a hand under the lace. Releasing her hair, he slipped his fingers beneath her sweater and yanked both fabrics down to her waist. He cupped her breasts, burying his face between her supple bosoms. His hot breath against her cool skin hardened her nipples.

Eyes closed and head still tilted backward, Elise savored the heat swirling down to her core. She envisioned the first time she kissed Deke and how just being close to him kicked up her pulse. Those passionate thoughts merged with Deke's physical touch, igniting an eruption about to explode between her thighs.

Deke unzipped her jeans and slid a hand inside her panties, his tongue still licking a hot path down her chest and stomach.

At the worst moment possible, her phone whirred, and whirred, and whirred, until she knew whoever was on the other end needed to talk immediately. "Deke. Let me turn off my phone. I'll remove my sweater, too."

He sighed and pushed away. "What a buzzkill. But now that you mention it, both of us are wearing way too much clothing." He grabbed his wine and downed the rest of the contents.

Elise stood and dug her phone from her pocket, then glanced at the screen.

Britt sent four texts, each with a similar message. *I know you're with Deke. Go somewhere private and call me...now.*

Heart pounding, Elise knew something was very wrong. Britt realized how important this weekend was. And why did she want to talk to Elise in private? Nonchalantly, so she wouldn't alert Deke, she tugged her camisole and sweater on instead of off. "Now that I'm up, I have to go to the bathroom. I'll change into something a little easier to manipulate, too."

Deke looked up, then stood. He drew her into an embrace. "I think you should just take everything off right here. Right now." He slid her hand over the bulge in his pants.

"I really have to go, Deke." She pulled away. "I'll be right back. I promise." She turned and ran up the stairs and into the master bathroom. Locking the door, she scrolled her phone to Britt's name, then pushed Call and quickly turned down the volume.

"Thank God." Britt's voice was laced with distress. "You're not near Deke, right?"

Elise turned on the faucet to create white noise. "He's downstairs. Why? What's so important?"

"I'm sending you a video. Don't hang up. Just watch it and keep the volume down so he can't hear."

"Britt, I hear your concern, but can't this wait until tomorrow? Deke and I were...uh...really busy."

"Yeah, Deke's busy all right. Look at the clip I just sent."

"Okay, okay." She flipped to her texts and opened Britt's post. The background music sounded like a party. Elise turned the volume lower and watched. Whoever recorded the clip must have been nervous. The shaky image and low lighting made the recording difficult to view with any certainty—until she saw Deke peer around the edge of the door. Her heart raced. Clearly inebriated, he was with a woman Elise didn't recognize, sucking her face. He kicked the door closed, then lifted her onto the bed. The session appeared to be consensual, because the woman lifted her skirt and pulled him close, then the video abruptly ended.

Elise felt sick to her stomach. She pushed the phone against her ear. "Where did you get this?"

"Remember Jade Seymore—the UGA cheerleader? She was a freshman when we were seniors, but her sister, Kayla—"

Trembling, Elise cut off Britt. "I remember Kayla. Was that Jade in the video?"

"No, hon. Jade was at a fraternity party last weekend and went upstairs to use the bathroom when she heard a couple outside the bedroom door. Realizing she'd have to walk right by them to return to the party, she peeked into the adjoining bedroom. That's when she saw Deke pressing the girl against the jamb. She knew he was engaged to you, so she recorded the incident, then sent the video to Kayla, who—"

"Who sent the recording to you, knowing you'd show it to me. Got it." A rush of adrenaline flushed over Elise. How could Deke do that to her? She sensed something was off, but this? This was beyond the pale. Damn. When it feels too good to be true.

"Sorry to dump this on you, hon, but I had to tell you before your romantic weekend. Your instincts were spot on when you felt something was wrong between you and Deke. It pissed me off he'd cheat on you and I had to let you know."

Bile swirled in Elise's stomach and stung as it choked into her throat. "That son of a—"

"For what it's worth, Elise, he fooled everyone."

"I guess, but that doesn't make his actions any easier to accept."

"Maybe now that he's set to be a big NFL star, he decided to play the role." Britt paused a long beat. "Are you okay? I mean, of course, you aren't okay, but what are you going to do?"

"I don't know. I'm still numb." A strong surge of fiery heat burned a path down her arms and legs. "I've got to go, Britt. Please, don't let anyone else see that video and ask Kayla and Jade to delete it. I'll call you later."

"Don't do anything crazy, Elise. He's not worth the trouble."

"Don't worry about me. We'll talk later." Elise ended the call. Still trembling, she splashed some water on her face, then patted it dry. Her thoughts spun, firing emotions that jumped from anger to betrayal to sadness to a hollow emptiness of complete and utter loss. If Deke could do what she saw with her own eyes, how could she ever trust him, or her own judgment, again?

She stuffed her phone into her back pocket, then turned off the faucet. As she approached the staircase, she had no idea what to say, but whatever she decided, she'd look him square in the eyes. He wasn't a drinker, and yet he'd had so much wine. She wanted him to leave, but she couldn't let him drive in that inebriated condition. One thing was for sure, she'd never let him touch her again. What she really needed was time to think.

Elise edged down three steps before she saw Deke standing in the open doorway, hands on his hips, buck-naked. "Deke." She darted down the steps toward him.

He spun and stared.

"What the hell are you doing?" Scowling, she nudged him aside and peered into the dark backyard. She knew no one was remotely close enough to see him standing there stark-naked, but still infuriated over the video, she justified her indignation.

"I simply opened the door. He zipped past me and tore off into the woods. I figured he'd just take a leak and come back."

She snapped a stare at him, her jaw dropped. "Jasper? Are you saying Jasper ran into the forest?"

He nodded. "Calm down, Elise. I'm sure he'll come back when he's ready. In the meantime, I removed the top of the hot tub. Let's have some fun."

Squeezing her hands into fists, she held back the emotion she wanted so badly to release. Instead, she plucked her jacket from a hook and pushed past him. "Get dressed, Deke." Then, turning her head, she scowled over her shoulder. "I'll be back when I find Jaz. Don't wait up." Anger seething, she ran across the yard into the dark   forest

Chapter Thirteen

Knowing the lay of the land helped her navigate in broad daylight, but Elise had never roamed the woods at night. Thank God, the moon provided some light, but through the dense forest, moonbeams did little more than cast eerie shadows off naked branches that danced with the cold March breeze. "Jaz. Here, boy." She flipped on her phone flashlight and shone the beam on the path before her.

Hiking through the woods, she couldn't stop thinking about Deke. She'd never let him see her cry. But now, outside, and out of range, she let down her stoic façade and tears streamed down her cheeks. A hollow sensation shuddered through her, shooting goosebumps down her arms. How could she have been so wrong about his character? No one saw this coming. Through high school and college, his choirboy reputation never faltered. Why now? And at a frat party? And with a cheerleader? Nothing about his behavior made sense.

Perhaps the idea of marriage suddenly felt too confining. But if that was the case, why didn't he just call off the engagement? Deke knew about her past and how hesitant she was to trust a man again. He swore he'd never hurt her. And yet, within hours after his indiscretion, he was ready, willing, and obnoxiously eager to have sex with Elise. A thought flashed to their earlier tryst and her stomach knotted again, pushing hot bile stinging into her throat.

A fury boiled inside her belly, and her muscles tensed. If she could be that wrong about Deke, she had no sense at all to judge the character of anyone. Not a great quality for a reporter. Suddenly, the idea of living a life interviewing athletes of any kind repulsed her. A lot of time would need to pass before she'd look into the face of a player without doubts of his real character.

Another rustling sounded in the distance, too large for a squirrel or fox. "Jasper. Here, boy." She slipped the phone under her arm and clapped her hands, then repeated the command, but her calls were met with silence. Aside from the crunch of leaves beneath her feet, the only sound she heard was the distant splash of water softly lapping against the shore as it clung to the edge of the lake, and night animals skittering by in search of food as they wandered through the underbrush. Why would Jasper take off like that? Elise had brought him to the lake on several occasions before, and she rarely used his leash. He never wandered far.

Deke was right about one thing. Jaz would return when he was ready. Elise knew her pup well. In truth, she was glad he ran off. In doing so, Jasper gave her the excuse she needed to get away from Deke, clear her head, and make sense of his strange behavior. . She needed distance to think. Without Deke. She also had a pretty good idea where Jasper went.

Whatever he'd seen in the woods earlier that afternoon interested him enough to want Elise to follow him. And she also knew, if whatever Jasper saw was dangerous, he'd have reacted very differently, barking, and growling with much more perseverance. At the time, Deke was Elise's priority. Now, not so much. So, she proceeded through the woods, using lake sounds and moonbeams to head in the right direction.

As the path narrowed, she pushed aside a dangling vine and shone the light ahead. Despite the creepy ambiance surrounding her, she knew this property and rarely—if ever—had she seen another person on this land. Many times, her father had taken her camping in these woods and taught her survival skills. She felt safe here.

Of course, a chance existed she might encounter some threatening wildlife…a fox, perhaps, or coyote…maybe even a bear. But, more often than not, if an animal saw her, they'd scoot in the opposite direction, especially with Jaz by her side. A thought occurred to her the rustling might be Deke, but in his current state, he'd likely fall asleep or pass out before following her into an unfamiliar forest. Again, she called out. "Jasper. Where are you, boy?" She continued her course.

A heartbeat later, Elise heard the scamper of a large animal rushing toward her through the leaves and underbrush. Her heart pounded. She turned off her flashlight...then stiffened...and held her breath, hoping the animal would pass by.

But the creature pounced directly in front of her. She froze, until her brain had a chance to catch up. "Oh, dear God, Jasper. You scared me to death." She breathed a long sigh of relief.

His wagging tail brushed against a bush, making a whoosh-whoosh sound.

Elise bent down and gave him a hug, then scrunched behind his ears. "Okay, Jaz, let's see what's so important out here that couldn't wait until tomorrow?"

He mouthed her sleeve and gave it a slight tug.

"You lead, buddy." She stood.

The dog released her arm, then scampered forward, veering off the beaten path.

Though the full moon shone brightly, tall trees and evergreens cast deep shadows, while branches and roots, still covered by a blanket of dry leaves, created a rough terrain for Elise to manipulate. She could no longer see Jaz, weaving in and out of the underbrush, but through the silence, she heard the rustling and forged forward. "Not so fast, Jaz. Slow down."

He paused, then woofed.

"Good boy." She followed Jaz for what felt like miles until the dense forest opened to a clearing, and a dark image appeared in the distance. Was the shadow a lean-to or hut of some kind? Elise had hiked this land too many times to count, but never had she seen a shack on her family's property. Perhaps the hike had taken her off course. Could she be lost? No. Even if she intended to, the chance of her reaching someone else's acreage on foot within an hour and in the dark was slim, at best.

She halted and studied the image. Then, softly whispering a call to Jaz, she edged forward. "Jasper. Come here."

Instead of obeying her command, he darted toward the hut, woofing as he approached.

The hairs on the back of Elise's neck stiffened. If someone was inside the structure, he—or she—definitely heard Jasper. She spun, ready to run into the woods should someone emerge from the hut, but a clanging sound made her freeze. Again, she turned and cautiously approached Jasper. The closer she go, the more curious she became.

Not only could she identify the odd shape was not a shack, but the noise continued with a rhythmic resonance, not a mechanical beat.

Jasper scratched at the tire of the eighteen-wheeler cab as if he was trying to dig his way into the truck.

"Jaz, no…heel, boy."

The moment she spoke, the clang stopped, and Jaz returned to her side.

"Is someone out there?"

The voice, though muffled, was familiar.

Thoughts spinning, Elise glanced at Jaz, then shifted her gaze to the truck. She climbed onto the footboard, then grasped the handle. To her surprise, the door wasn't locked. Instead, it flew open, pushing her off the step. Again, she climbed up, this time clutching the handle before yanking open the door.

"Thank God." He pounded on the panel. "Please. Can you hear me?"

Evaluating the situation before she spoke, Elise said nothing. She glared at the steel compartment built in behind the driver and passenger seats, then stepped between them. Searching for a knob, she ran a hand over the edges of the cold metal. She saw only a padlock locking the panels together. The middle segment had to open. She inspected the edges, then slowly raised her gaze...perhaps upward into the truck's ceiling. On further examination, she noticed a slide-open peephole of sorts about a foot wide and an inch or two high.

"Dear God, don't leave me here. I've been abducted."

She flipped the catch. Stunned, Elise drew back her head. Squeezing her brows together, she stared in shock.

"Please." He pounded again. "Help me get out of here before he returns."

Hand trembling, she slowly slid open the tiny panel and peered inside. A shot of heat stabbed through her. Lips trembling and racked in fear, she tried to ask what happened. But only one word came—"Deke?"

Chapter Fourteen

Pounding on the exterior wall, Deke Madigan prayed the owner of the dog woofing and scratching outside heard the clatter. He knew the tiny room imprisoning him had to be some sort of mobile home or RV, but his captor took care to park the vehicle in remote areas. For weeks, every time his abductor left, Deke beat against the side panel, hoping someone would hear, but no one came to his rescue.

This time, he could swear he heard a woman's voice in the distance. His fist sore from pummeling against the wall, he grabbed the one pan he had and smacked it against the steel. *Please, God, let someone hear me*.

He paused to listen and heard footsteps approaching. "Is someone out there?" Again, he listened for a response and heard the driver's side door open. "Thank God." He beat on the partition, praying his captor wasn't the person on the other side. "Please. Can you hear me?" His heart racing, he feared the person abandoned him.

He yelled at the top of his lungs, "Dear God, don't leave me here. I've been abducted." Again, he pounded on the wall. "Please. Help me get out of here before he returns."

The small opening in the wall slid to the side. "Deke?"

The voice he heard had him questioning if he'd died and gone to heaven. "Elise?" Was she here, or was his solitude finally turning him stark raving mad? He shoved his head against the panel so he could see through the viewer. "Oh my God––Elise? Am I dreaming? How did you find me?" His pulse kicked up into overdrive. Where had his captor taken him that Elise could be here? The thought caused his heart to race. "You've got to get out of here. This guy is crazy. Can––"

"Slow down, Deke. One thing at a time. How did you lock yourself in this semi?"

"Semi? I'm locked in the sleeper cab of an eighteen-wheeler container? I thought this was some kind of RV."

She took hold of the padlock and tugged, then scratched her head. "How the hell did you lock yourself inside?"

Jasper jumped between the driver and passenger seats, then scratched at the steel panel, woofing feverishly.

Deke peered downward through the view slot. "Good boy, Jaz. But please, shush."

Jaz immediately responded to his voice and quieted then stood on his back paws and peered at Deke.

95

"Good boy." He stroked Jasper's nose, then gazed at Elise. "If he hears Jaz barking, he'll come running."

Elise frowned. "He who?"

"The guy who locked me in this place. He's certifiable, Elise. I don't know what he'd do if he sees you here. How in the world did you find me?"

"I didn't. You can thank Jaz for that."

"Jaz. I could have sworn I heard his bark earlier today, but I figured it was just wishful thinking. How are you here? Where are we?" Thoughts spinning, Deke tried to make sense of the situation, but with his captor close by, no time existed to figure out details. The man could return at any moment. Sooner or later, Deke would have a chance to escape. But Elise was in real danger. He had to get her to leave.

"This truck cab is parked in the woods about a mile from the lake house." Her stare bored into his. "I knew you were drun—"

"Listen to me, Elise. Exchanging details won't help right now. The man who locked me in here could return any minute. You're in grave danger."

She harrumphed and shook her head. "Ha. I don't know where this truck came from or how you locked yourself in there, and to be honest, I really don't care. You can rot there for all I care."

Her comment burned through him like a hot knife slicing butter. "What? I mean, why? I didn't plan this abduction. Why are you so enraged?"

A blank stare skewed her features. "What are you talking about?"

"Listen, Elise, I have no idea how long I've been in this hellhole, but I'd have thought, after weeks missing, you'd at least be happy to see me."

"Weeks missing?" Her gaze shot daggers. "I don't know what game you're playing, Deke. And frankly, I don't give a damn. But I have every right to be angry. If you didn't want to marry me, you could have at least told me face to face."

"Hold on. What are you talking about?" Stoked with adrenaline, he felt like their discussion was on two completely different channels. How was he not getting through to her?

After fumbling for something in a pocket, she stepped back and scrolled through her phone. A moment later, she held the screen in front of the view slot and started a video.

Completely stunned by the recording, he dropped his jaw. "Huh? What the hell? How did you get that video?"

"I thought so," she snapped back. "You're busted." She yanked away her cell and ended the display. "How I came across proof of your little tryst is irrelevant." She stuffed the phone into her pocket and turned toward the door. "So, you'll excuse me if I don't rush to your rescue."

"Wait, Elise. That's not me."

"Right. I suppose it's your long-lost identical twin brother? You're so lame."

Her reaction pummeled him like a gut punch, and his stomach twisted into knots, spewing bitterness into his throat. What the hell? "Elise. You have to believe me. I know that video looks damning, but I swear on all that is holy, the man in that recording is not me. I've been locked in this truck for weeks."

She let out a clearly sarcastic snicker. "Really, Deke. You've played me for a fool long enough. I don't know how you got locked inside that cab, or how the damn truck ended up on my property, but I'm beyond caring. Find your own way out. I'm done." She stepped onto the footboard.

"Elise, stop. Please." He kicked the steel panel, sending a stab of pain from his bare toes through his foot and into his ankle. "If you've ever loved me, at least hear me out."

Elise spun and scowled. "You really have the balls to say you're not the guy screwing that cheerleader? Humph. I'm not that gullible."

"That's exactly what I'm saying. You've got to believe me. Anyone could have made that recording."

"True. But not anyone could star in it. And why would someone take the time to record a fake video of you?"

"I don't know, and I don't know why anyone would kidnap me and hold me hostage for weeks in this truck, either. But someone did."

She stepped farther into the cab. "Are you trying to gaslight me, or are you still drunk?"

Deke squinted. "You know I don't drink, Elise. I've never admitted why to anyone, but in truth, alcohol makes me violently sick. It has ever since Papaw caught me and Matt drinking behind his garage one night. He made us down enough to cause us to puke our guts. If you don't believe me, ask Matt."

"Okay. Assuming someone jumped you, how could he get the upper hand? You're in the best condition of your life, Deke." She moved closer to the opening. Peering into the room, she inspected him from head to foot. "At least, you were."

"Exactly. I *was* in the best condition—and if I'm forced to eat another peanut butter and honey sandwich, I'll scream—but my point is, I've been cooped up in this prison for weeks. And you want to know how? The bastard snuck up behind me when I was in the shower and knocked me out."

"You mean some guy broke into your apartment and—"

"No. I was in the locker room at the Combine."

Her brow wrinkled. "You mean you've been locked in this truck since the Combine? That's impossible." She frowned.

"I'm telling you the truth. The guy crept behind me in the shower and wrapped an arm around my neck in a chokehold. The next thing I remember was waking up here." He took a few steps backward. "Look at this room. All the creature comforts of an emergency bunker. A toilet, sink, and small shower, a cabinet of food, water, a bed with sheets and a blanket, even a pair or two of sweats and a lousy toothbrush. But no windows, no television, or clock. I'm completely isolated from the outside world. Hell, in here, I have no way of knowing if it's day or night."

She squinted and drew her brows together, slightly parting her lips.

Her stunned expression told him she was beginning to believe his explanation. "What I don't get is why he locked me in this room. Why not just kill me?"

Her eyes went wide. "God, don't even mention killing."

"I have to. Think about it, Elise. He's holding me here—alive—for a reason. And if that reason disappears, I'm pretty sure I will, too, permanently."

She shivered. A grimace washed over her face.

He could almost see her thoughts spinning. "Why would someone abduct me, then drive around with me in tow?"

"If someone really did kidnap you, surely a worker at the Combine complex would have seen something." Elise slowly sat against the driver's side arm. Her forehead wrinkled.

"Not likely. Matt came by while I was showering. Before he left, he said everyone was gone and ribbed me for being the last to leave—again. The guy took me down, I'm not proud of that, but he did. Though, I'm not sure how he carried me from the locker room to this truck."

"Okay. I'll play along for a few minutes and accept you're telling the truth. Anyone who's ever watched crime TV could answer that dilemma. If you were out cold, the perp probably just heaved you into one of those laundry carts for towels in the locker rooms. Then, he simply rolled you out of the building."

"That makes sense. Elise, you've got to believe me. He's dangerous. And if he discovers you found me, you'll become a target, too. You have to get out of here before he comes back."

She gazed at Jasper, now curled into the passenger seat. "What do you think, boy? Is this guy telling us the truth?"

Jasper let out two woofs, then wagged his tail.

"The man who abducted you. What did he look like?"

Deke scratched his head. "I don't know. Honestly, I haven't actually seen the guy. Only his eyes. On the rare occasions he opens the viewer to give me something. But he talks when he drives. I'm not sure if he mutters to me or himself, but God, his droning voice makes my skin crawl."

"Come on, Deke. You had to have gotten a glimpse of him when he jumped you."

"I've been racking my brain to remember. The night he abducted me is so sketchy. One minute I was rinsing the soap from my hair, and a blink later, an arm wrapped around my neck and squeezed until I blacked out. Even if the guy had attacked from the front, between shampoo suds and shower streams, my vision was too blurred to identify anyone. For a brief moment, I thought I saw his reflection in the wall mirror. But" — challenging his memory, he rubbed his fingertips on the center of his forehead in a circular motion, then raised his gaze to meet Elise's. He shook his head—"the   face   I   saw   was   mine."

Chapter Fifteen

Thoughts spinning, Deke paced the tiny room. For the life of him, he had no idea why this man targeted him. Or what if…could his target be Elise? He didn't want to scare her, but the possibility existed. If only he could remember the man's face.

He shrugged. "I know that's impossible. But when I close my eyes and really try to visualize that night, I only see myself in the locker room. No one else. Maybe the trauma or shock suppressed my memory."

"Okay, let's rethink this. You say you've been locked in this rig since a guy kidnapped you from the Combine locker room, right?"

He nodded. "I'm not sure how long ago that was. Weeks for sure. Maybe a month? Damn. Time is meaningless in here. I don't have a frickin' calendar, and with no windows, I can't even tell if it's day or night." He frowned. "How long have I been missing?"

She blew out a soft puff of air. "That's the problem, Deke. And why your story is so hard to believe."

"What are you talking about?"

"You never went missing. In fact—" Her stare intensified, as if her thoughts clarified something. "I was with you at the cabin." Her voice softened. "Less than an hour ago."

"What? No way."

Elise's gaze lowered. "At least, I thought he was you." After a long pause, she peered directly into his eyes. "Could someone be impersonating you?"

He drew back and scratched the stubble on his chin as her comment sank in. Why would someone want to take his place? Why would his abductor bring him to Elise's Lake Lanier property? He must have parked the truck cab close enough to the cabin to keep an eye on Deke, but far enough away to make it impossible to hear Deke's cries for help. But if Elise wasn't his target, why involve her? Perhaps for leverage? Could Deke possess or know something his double sought? If so, he might threaten to hurt Elise to obtain what he needed. No. If his double wanted something, he would have already laid out demands.

Deke's attention refocused on Elise. God, she was so beautiful. He missed her so much. An ache lodged beneath his sternum. His biggest fear leapt from his own safety to hers. He could tell her curiosity flew into overdrive by the look on her face. And he knew, once she set her mind on something, she wouldn't let go until she had answers. He'd always attributed that asset to her journalistic curiosity. But now, the attribute had become a liability. "Seriously, Elise. You have to leave before it's too late."

"Wait a minute." Her brow wrinkled and her lips pooched to the side. "What if your memory is spot-on? What if you couldn't visualize the reflection of the guy who abducted you, because he was you. I mean, what if he looked exactly like you? I think the reflection you saw in the mirror was your double."

"What? I don't have a twin. That's impossible."

"Considering I just left you at my cabin, the premise makes perfect sense. If—and that is a huge if—you're telling the truth, someone has taken your place. Someone who has gone to great lengths. Maybe to be a first-round draft pick?"

Angling his head, he pinched his eyebrows together. "That might make sense in a twisted sort of way. If I wasn't missing, no one would be looking for me. So, you think the guy who's holding me captive took my place. But how could he slide into my life, and why?"

"Plastic surgery can perform miracles these days." She shook her head. "That could explain a lot. But how could he act exactly like you and know what you know? The thought never occurred to doubt you weren't you. Who does that?"

"I have to say, the guy I thought was you gave me no reason to question your identity. He lives in your apartment, has your phone and wallet, and knows everything about you. If he could fool me, he could easily fool everyone else." She dropped her gaze toward Jasper. "Except Jaz." She ran a hand over his soft blond fur. "You knew, didn't you, boy?"

"How would Jaz know?"

"For weeks, Jasper has acted really odd around you. I mean, the other you. He growled, never jumped up on your lap or licked your face, and he doesn't bring toys to play with the imposter like he does you. In fact, the only time Jaz settles down around the fake Deke is when he gives him a dog biscuit and, even then, he backs off to eat the treat. Why didn't I connect the dots?"

"Dogs can sense things people can't. He knew that imposter wasn't me, even though he looks like me." Deke pressed his head against the cold steel and peered through the viewer toward Jasper. "Didn't you, boy?"

Jaz stood and raised his paws to the viewer, then gave Deke several slobbery licks.

"See, Jaz knows I'm me. That's got to prove to you I'm the real Deke Madigan."

"Yeah. As weird as this whole situation is, I think I'm starting to believe you. Now that I think about it, I saw so many signs. The odd remarks, and" —she snapped a gaze to Deke—"What's your favorite vegetable?"

"What? Why?"

"Just humor me, Deke."

"You already know the answer to that question. Brussels sprouts, but they have to be crispy."

"I rest my case."

He pressed a hand on the divider. "You believe me?"

"I'm definitely leaning in that direction."

"Then you see why it's so important you get out of here. Go back to the cabin and don't let him know you're on to him."

"I'm pretty sure he's sleeping and will be out for a while. He drank more than a bottle of wine. Besides, we've got to get you out of here." She ran a hand around the panel, then stopped at the padlock.

"I've tried everything. There's no way out of this hellhole. I think he designed this whole sleeper cab for the sole purpose of kidnapping me. But what I can't figure out is why."

She shrugged. "I don't know but realizing fake Deke at my place isn't you explains a lot."

"You said that before. What do you mean?"

She bit the corner of her lower lip. "I thought my anxiety was all in my head. I rationalized I was just freaked out about the murder."

Deke's eyes went wide. "Murder? What murder?"

Her gaze lowered to the floor for a long beat before returning to meet his.

"Come on, Elise. I know you. When you bite your bottom lip, I know you're really worried."

She pressed her lips together, then smiled. "You really are my Deke. Not the lying bastard in my cabin. Thank God."

"Finally. Now, tell me about the murder."

"A woman in my condo complex. But that's not important now."

He took a step back and wrung his hands, pacing the width of the small room. "You don't know that. What if the woman in your complex saw something that might have exposed him? I have no doubt my double is capable of murder." The thought of how close the guy was to Elise prickled the hairs on the back of his neck and twisted his stomach. "So, what did you mean when you said that explains a lot?"

"My gut feelings were right all along. Now, I understand why I felt weird around him at times. Why his touch made me feel creepy, why he drank so much and didn't like Brussels sprouts."

Deke laughed. "That's a helluva tell. A lot of people don't like Brussels sprouts."

"But you love them. He really tried to take your place, but he wasn't you."

Deke lowered his gaze to his bare feet. "He gave me basic needs, but never shoes. I wonder why?"

"Maybe he didn't anticipate you wear different sizes."

Deke returned his gaze to Elise. "Either that, or he figured if I ever managed to escape, I wouldn't get far barefoot. I assume he had access to my apartment and clothing. Does he dress like me? What was he wearing at the cabin tonight?"

She chuckled. "The last time I saw him…nothing. He was buck-naked."

"Shit." He pounded a fist on the steel panel, then yanked it back in pain. "That son of a bitch." He glared through the viewer. "If he touched a hair on your head—"

"I'm fine. And we never slept together. Not since the Combine." She ran a hand over the cold steel until her fingers wrapped around the padlock again. She yanked hard. "We need to get you out of here, Deke."

"Yes. And quickly. I'm telling you, Elise. That guy is crazy. He talks to himself and says irrational things. If he finds out you know he's not the real Deke Madigan, he might—"

"Then we can't let him know I'm on to him. I wonder why he'd go to the trouble of plastic surgery to take over your life?"

"After listening to him for the last few weeks, I'm pretty sure his life sucks. But I don't know why he chose me."

"Are you kidding? An NFL football star. Isn't that every boy's dream?"

He raked a hand through his hair. "I suppose that fantasy is right up there. But he'll have to perform to stay on the team. I've worked my ass off to get there. Even if he's athletic and can throw a ball, he won't be able to compete in the NFL."

"Who knows what lurks in the mind of a madman?" Again, she tugged on the padlock, then searched through the console, glove compartment, and under the seats. "He must have the key with him. To get you out of here, I have to go back to the cabin."

"No, Elise." A pang of sheer terror coursed through his veins. "Your plan is too dangerous. You don't know what that guy is capable of."

"I'll be careful. But I can't get you out of here without a key, or at least something to cut off the padlock. I'm pretty sure my dad has something in his shed to slice through the lock. I'll be back as soon as I can."

Again, the knot in his stomach twisted. "Why don't you call 911? I'm sure they can get me out of here."

"I would, but if the guy is a psychopath, he won't react rationally. He might take me captive if the police show up, and there's no way they could get close enough without Daddy's alarm sounding—which I armed after Deke—I mean, your imposter arrived. If the police turn down the road to our cabin, they'll trip the alarm. We have to catch fake Deke completely by surprise. Besides, I want to be sure you're free and safe before we bring in the police."

"I'm not concerned about myself, Elise. Given the chance, I know I can take him. Now that he thinks he has succeeded, he'll slip up. When he does, I'll escape."

"Since you're locked up at the moment, you have no choice but to do things my way. But don't worry. Your double obviously wants me in the picture. He's been good to me, so I think we're safe as long as he thinks everyone believes he's you."

Deke reached a hand through the viewer and brushed a finger over her cheek. "I love you, Elise Sloan. Please, be careful. If anything happens to you, I—"

"Nothing will happen to us. Come on, Jaz." She clapped her hands together twice.

Jasper immediately followed, then halted. Turning, he stared at the truck, barked, then bolted into the cab.

"Go with Elise, Jaz. I'll be fine. You need to protect her." Deke had no idea how much Jasper understood, but the dog's intelligence continually amazed him.

Jaz returned to Elise, but he hesitated several times, peering over his shoulder toward Deke.

"Good boy." Elise called out to Deke, "Just sit tight. I promise I'll come back when I find the key or something to break the lock." She gazed at Jasper. "This time, we'll take the path, boy. It's shorter and much easier. Heel."

Jasper followed her command.

Deke watched Elise until she disappeared from the viewer. No longer could he sit back and wait for an opportunity to escape. Every moment Elise spent near his double heightened her danger. The guy might be stone-cold crazy, but he was smart, and he clearly thought out every detail of Deke's abduction. If Elise slipped up one time, he'd turn on her in a heartbeat. Deke couldn't let that happen. To keep her safe, he had to escape—now. But   how?

Chapter Sixteen

Daryl glared as Elise jogged into the dark forest, yelling for Jasper. He knew the mutt would be a problem from day one but straying from his plan presented a greater risk. At least, he subdued the mongrel's hostility with dog biscuits. Of course, wearing Madigan's clothes didn't hurt, either, but the dog knew something was off and remained cautious. If push came to shove, he'd get rid of the dog. For two years, Daryl had memorized every detail about his mark. If he could fool Elise, he could fool the world. And no mutt would stand in the way of his success.

He strolled toward the hot tub, then slid into the warm, bubbling water. Tilting his head onto the edge of the spa, he stared at the stars sparkling against the dark velvet sky. This was the life he'd dreamed of since he was a child. A life his momma told him could be his if he worked hard in school. And he did. He sat at the front of the class, studied every subject, completed all his homework, and made good grades.

When the other kids played outside, Daryl sat and studied in the back room of wherever his momma worked, the truck stop, then the diner. But, when Momma started working as a custodian in the Calvary General Hospital, she said Doc Wilson noticed her interest in the patients and thought she looked familiar. Turned out, she'd met him when she first came to town. Daryl was too young to remember, though. But the doc hired her as an assistant and a few years later, she'd saved enough money for a down payment on their little house.

Yeah, Daryl worked hard, all right. He swore one day he'd be better than the kids who called him trailer trash. Unfortunately, when his momma fell sick, he lost his chance to go to college. He dropped out of school and worked his butt off to pay the bills. He didn't blame her. She was a good mother, and he knew she did her best. But sometimes, doing your best wasn't good enough. Anger seethed inside at the thought of his childhood. His muscles tightened and his fingers curled into clenched fists. Daryl wouldn't let anyone stand in his way. Even if he had to commit murder to stop them.

Having searched every inch of his prison for weeks, Deke had found nothing he could use to assist in his escape. Sifting through the drawer next to the sink, he found a single set of plastic silverware, a plastic package of paper plates, a box of crackers, a jar of peanut butter, a squeeze bottle of honey, a box of cereal, a salt and pepper shaker, instant coffee with one cup, and three loaves of bread—which he moved to the fridge to keep them from growing moldy. The small fridge held two dozen eggs, a hunk of cheese, two sticks of butter, a big plastic jar of nuts. But no milk for cereal or coffee.

The drawer beneath the pull-down bed held two pairs of boxers, a t-shirt, a sweatshirt with matching pants, one toothbrush and a tube of toothpaste, an electric shaver, a towel, and washcloth, and three rolls of toilet paper.

His double was definitely smart. Plastic silverware gave Deke nothing to pry open any part of the room. The flat-surfaced electric stove had two burners. One held a frying pan, and the other a pot. Little chance of catching anything on fire.

Peanut butter and honey sandwiches with eggs weren't conducive to staying in shape, and he knew his current condition fell far short of what he'd been at the Combine, despite the pushups, sit-ups, and old-fashioned calisthenics he kept up daily when his captor wasn't around. He worked out not only to maintain some semblance of his training for after he escaped, but also to make sure his physical fitness stayed well beyond that of his nemesis.

Though his meager food kept him alive, what concerned him was when the food ran out. His captor had yet to show his face—which Elise described as his double—let alone offer to bring him a damn thing above what he'd already provided. Deke had the sinking feeling that his days were numbered. Yet, for some reason, this guy wanted him alive, at least, so far. Now that Deke knew he was close to Elise's cabin and the creep had taken over his life, and fiancée, the stakes skyrocketed. Not that she wasn't one of the smartest and most resourceful women he'd ever known, but the guy was certifiable, and Deke didn't want Elise anywhere near the man.

His thoughts spun around what might happen when Elise returned, and he froze first on an embrace. If that maniac touched her, he cringed at the thought. A burning knot twisted in Deke's belly, shooting a wave of fiery heat down his arms and legs. To protect Elise, Deke had to escape— sooner than later. He'd exhausted every idea over the weeks he'd spent in this living hell. No way out existed, and that was unacceptable.

He squeezed his fists, tensing every muscle in his body, then let out a bloodcurdling howl. "Ahhhhhhhhhhh." Losing all control, Deke kicked the steel walls, then spun, tossing, punching, and kicking everything around the entire room. After at least a two-minute bout against his prison, he calmed and gazed around, concluding he'd accomplished exactly nothing aside from crumpling the few life-saving necessities he had. He collapsed onto the bed, emotionally and physically drained. "Dear God, please help me save Elise."

As if in answer to his prayer, the grill once affixed over the heat and air unit controls dangled against the wall, then fell to the floor.

Chuckling, Deke shook his head and peered toward the ceiling. "Not exactly what I was asking for."

He stood, then leaned over and picked up the metal casing. Inspecting the grill, he attempted to reattach the metal so his captor wouldn't miss the protector but thought better of the idea. Maybe he could manipulate the metal to create some kind of tool. He might be able to pry something. Again, he gazed around the tiny room. Pry what? Nothing existed in this room that was remotely pry-able. Sick and tired of spending weeks caged and at the whims of his captor, Deke felt his blood boil and pump into his neck. *Damn.* His captor had thought of everything, down to the last detail.

He slammed a fist against the wall, hitting the AC control dead center, and a sharp pain shot up his arm. At the same moment, the truck shuddered, and the back panels slid apart into a hideaway wall to reveal a black curtain. His gaze shifted to the AC controls. He wiggled the box, then touched the Off button and the back panel began to close. Immediately, he shoved a thumb against the On button. When the panels separated, a rush of heat swirled from his core and shot to his hands and feet. A sense of hope pounded his heart so hard he could hear the beat.

Edging toward the curtain, he paused and listened, then hooked a finger and pulled aside the thick fabric to see—*Holy crap.* He could scarcely believe what he saw. Hidden behind the steel panels and a heavy curtain, a door now stood between Deke and his freedom. He twisted the handle, and the latch responded, opening into the dark night. *Thank you, Lord.* He was finally free. He peered outside then cautiously placed a foot onto the trailer hitch.

Listening to the nocturnal sounds of the forest, he scanned the area before stepping off the truck. Barefoot and lost, at least now he had a fighting chance to find the cabin and help Elise. But which way should he go? If he could locate the lake, he could watch the current to get his bearings. But he heard no lapping water to guide his way. *Think, Deke.* He knew the cabin was within walking distance. Had Elise said anything to give him an idea of which way to go? Her voice came from the driver's side of the truck, but that told him nothing. Surrounded by deep forest, he gazed toward the sky. The full moon shone brightly, casting shadows through the trees.

He snapped his fingers. "That's it." He remembered Elise talking to Jasper. The last thing she said was, "This time, we'll take the path, boy. It's shorter and much easier." He spun, searching for a small opening or break from the dense forest. *There.*

Heart pounding, he rushed toward the path dimly lit by moonbeams, but the ground, covered in damp leaves, pine straw, vines, and underbrush bit at his bare feet. He'd have to stride slowly and watch where he stepped. Injuring a foot, at the very least, would slow his pace, and at worst, would prevent him from finding the cabin. That was not an option.

The damp ground chilled his toes. Striding carefully, he reached a path about seven feet wide and a bit more worn, which eased his already pain-stricken feet. He diligently picked up his pace and shook his head at his double's clever plan. Disguising a panic button as an air conditioning and heat control. Deke never doubted the man's intelligence or attention to detail. As crazy as the guy was, he had a shrewd mind...so ingenious he included a failsafe...an escape switch safeguard in the event he accidentally trapped himself—or his mark got the upper hand and locked him inside his own panic room.

Deke still didn't understand why he was the man's mark. A lot of more high-profile, valuable, and rich victims existed. He shrugged, continuing his trek toward the cabin. He needed to outsmart his double. He wouldn't know the situation until he arrived, but he still needed a plan. Probably a backup strategy, as well.

Deep in thought, he lifted his gaze toward the moon and felt a sharp stab on the pad of his left foot. He staggered to the side of the path and collapsed onto a fallen tree. *Damn!* He shouldn't have looked away from the trail. He inspected the wound and yanked out a large sliver of wood under his big toe. Realizing the warm, sticky fluid was blood, he reached behind his perch for a handful of leaves to wipe the injury, but the prickly stubble he felt instead made his skin crawl. Spinning, he caught a glimpse of what he'd touched and jerked from his seat to stare into the cold, unshaven blue-gray face of an old man.

Chapter Seventeen

Glancing at his shriveled fingers, Daryl reluctantly stood, then stepped over the edge of the hot tub and went inside. The logs in the fireplace, burned to embers, now glowed a reddish orange. He snatched a blanket draped over an easy chair and dried off, then slipped into his boxers and t-shirt and knelt by the fireside. After adding two logs, he stoked the fire until it burst into flames, then sat and stared at the blaze, mesmerized by the flicker casting shadows that danced across the wall. For two years, he'd planned his revenge, but he never realized how sweet retribution would feel. He finally had the life he dreamed of...the life he deserved. He wished his momma was alive to see how clever he was.

Of course, she'd be appalled he committed murder. She lived by the mantra, *first do no harm.* For most of his life, Daryl had lived a studious, silent existence. As a loner, compliant and timid as a boy, he trusted his mother's guidance and looked up to her and the doc. He was the perfect child.

But the promise she and the doc made never panned out, and once he learned the truth about his past, he felt as if his life was a lie.

Perhaps his momma felt she was protecting him when she said his father and grandparents died. Keeping them dead in her own mind might have eased her pain, but she deprived Daryl from knowing his roots, not to mention what might have been a large inheritance. His heart hardened when he learned how her parents disowned her, and his once-kind soul filled with vengeance and rage. Not against his momma, but toward her family and the despicable men who stole her virtue.

Obsessed with finding and confronting his biological father, he studied genetics and DNA retrieval techniques. He doubted any of the gang would simply hand over their DNA, especially if they knew why he wanted the sample. So, he learned the basics to find out himself. Then, he plugged into genetic genealogy to search his ancestry. Narrowing down the truth took time and patience, but he dug deeply and found that using DNA phenotyping and genetic genealogy, he could enter his DNA into the genetic database for possible relative matches. All he needed was access, which he found hacking into the doc's computer files. But he never expected to find that the Madigan family fit into the fray. With three possible prospects in hand, Daryl decided to shelf his paternal search briefly to turn his attention to Deke Madigan.

Again, Daryl flashed on his momma. She'd definitely be impressed with his work, but not the murders. Damn. He never intended to off that woman. He just panicked...and he hadn't meant to kill the caretaker, either. That was an accident. They were in the wrong place at the wrong time.

All Daryl wanted to do was find a nice, quiet, secure place to park his cab. The Sloan lake property was perfect. Especially since he could use Elise as an excuse for being there. If the caretaker had just minded his own business, he wouldn't have heard Deke clanging in the back of his truck. It wasn't Daryl's fault. Sure, he shoved the man and told him to mind his own business. How did he know the guy would trip and hit his head on a rock?

Now, he was a fugitive. Thank goodness he switched lives with Deke. If he hadn't, he'd likely land in prison. The only loose end was Madigan.

When the latch turned on the back door, he turned his head and froze—until he saw Elise. "Wow. It took you a long time to find Jasper." He stood and stretched. "I was beginning to worry about you." He sat, then patted the sofa beside him. "You must be chilled to the bone. Come sit beside me and warm up."

"I uh...think I'll run upstairs and take a quick shower. I had to trek through the woods, and I feel like I have spiders crawling all over me."

Again, he stood and lifted his eyebrows. "That sounds like fun. Can I join you and wash your back?"

She turned toward the stairway and gazed upward to see Jasper watching her every move from his favorite perch. "No. I just want to wash off the prickly feeling. You stay here and enjoy the fire. I'll be down in a few minutes."

He squinted, assessing her demeanor and body language. "Okay. Suit yourself, sweet pea. But I promise you'd enjoy every minute." He chuckled.

Elise called out over her shoulder, "I'm sure I would. I'll take a raincheck."

The one wild card in Daryl's plan was Elise. He knew her background meant she'd have the prissy, rich girl attitude he detested, but he was pleasantly surprised when he stepped into Deke's life. She was sexy, sweet, and nothing like the women he'd known in the past. He wouldn't mind a bit having her by his side, as long as she was as hot in bed as he assumed she'd be. One way or the other, he planned to find out tonight.

If she gave him any grief along the way, he'd simply drop her like a hot potato. He didn't need her daddy's money. He'd have all he wanted with an NFL contract. Besides, he'd already taken a taste of the wild women who drooled all over Deke Madigan. Daryl could have his pick, or maybe a different one every night. Elise was damn lucky to have his full attention, and if she somehow managed to uncover his secret...he'd killed before, but never intentionally. He wondered if he could kill her with malice and forethought. He thought not. She was a good woman. As long as he treated her well and kept her from discovering the truth, they'd be blissfully happy.

Trembling, Elise calmly ascended the stairs
Trembling, Elise calmly ascended the stairs toward
the master suite, then softly closed the door behind
her. She turned on the shower, then sifted through
Deke's—no, the imposter's—bags, searching
desperately for his truck keys. One thing was for
sure, he didn't have them on him...and he had to
have them close. If she couldn't find them in his
overnight duffle bag, she'd have to check his car.
That might prove to be a little tricky. Deke usually
carried the keyless entry fob in a pocket. Would
the imposter do the same? If so, she'd have to
rummage through his jeans. But one step at a
time.

Digging a hand into his bag, she searched
every pocket, including those in his clothing.
Nothing. *Damn!* She'd have to move to step two.
After carefully replacing his possessions exactly as
he'd left them, she stripped and stepped under the
rain shower. Never had she gone through any
semblance of the emotions she'd experienced in
the last twenty-four hours. How could she have
ever assumed the man downstairs was Deke? Her
neck clenched as she recalled kissing him. She
tried to convince herself nothing had changed. But
everything changed. And yet, she rationalized
each red flag as her own issue.

"Pah." She spat out the sour taste of his kiss, then scrubbed her face. As much as she wanted to get as far away from him as possible, she knew in order to find his keys and return to Deke, she'd have to let him kiss her and hold her close. The thought of his hands fondling her made her stomach roil. But she had to fake whatever was needed to save Deke.

Scrubbing her skin to wash off the filth, she thought about what she needed to protect herself if double-trouble sensed something was off. She wasn't sure if he was capable of murder, but she had to consider the possibility. Her father kept a gun in a hideaway drawer behind the bedside table. Before she returned to the imposter downstairs, she'd check to make sure the cylinder was loaded. If not, she knew Dad kept additional cartridges, but where?

Her father had taught Elise how to shoot his gun when she was eight, and they often went into the woods for target practice over the years. At first, she thought it odd he wanted his daughter to learn how to shoot and wondered if he might have wished for a son, instead. She smiled, remembering how adamant he was when she questioned his motive.

"I prayed for a girl I could hug, kiss, and spoil. From the moment I saw you, Elise, you were the light of my life." He drew her close and had squeezed her. "I hope you never need a gun, but I want to be sure you will always be safe. That's why I'm teaching you how to shoot."

She stepped from the stall and dried off, then slipped into a pair of flannel lounge pants and a long-sleeved t-shirt. To make sure the imposter wouldn't walk in on her checking the gun, she strode into the hall and gazed over the banister. "Hey, Deke." It flipped her stomach to call him Deke, but she forced the bile down and continued. "Would you mind pouring me another glass of wine? I think there's more in the bottle on the kitchen counter."

"Sure, sweet pea. I think I'll pour another for me, too."

How did he know Deke's pet names for her? And the white rose he gave her for no occasion except to say he was thinking of her. He knew so many details about Deke's life—and hers. Why did he choose to steal Deke's life? She turned away and rolled her eyes. "I'll be down in a minute. I can get another bottle from the wine cellar if we need one."

"I'll be waiting."

She shuddered at the thought of what she knew he expected from her, then returned to the bedroom. When she pressed the hidden button, the secret drawer dropped to reveal the revolver. She checked to make sure the chambers were loaded. Yes. Good. She closed the cylinder, returned the gun to the drawer, and pushed it closed. Heart racing, she slowly stepped down the stairs.

Chapter Eighteen

With each descending step, Elise felt her pulse kick up a beat. She glanced at Jaz, perched in his favorite spot, and splayed her hand, commanding him to stay put. After a quick glance around the great room, she ricocheted to the dining room, searching for the jeans Deke wore earlier that evening. His keys had to be in a pocket of those pants. Wait, when she left to find Jasper, he was standing in the open doorway, naked. Maybe he disrobed in the bathroom, or by the spa.

At the bottom of the stairs, she glanced upward toward Jaz, now peering through the hallway banister. He didn't trust Deke's double, but he didn't stray far from her, either. Turning toward the fireplace, she drew in a long breath. She had to pull this off, even if the man sitting by the fireside now repulsed her. If he thought she knew something, would he become violent? And if so, how far would he go? She'd seen no signs of violence and no temper since the switch. As long as she played the game, he'd have no reason to hurt her.

"Hey, beautiful. Come sit." He patted the seat next to him.

The fire blazed and the ambiance was drenched in romance. Exactly what she planned. How could she keep him at arm's length without arousing his curiosity about her one-eighty? Arousing, the very thought of the word associated with this impersonator made her blood boil. She strolled toward him, then sat and snuggled close, the anger in her stomach churning.

"Sorry about letting Jasper out without a leash. I didn't think he'd run off like that."

She gazed at him through her eyelashes. "It wasn't your fault. I'm just glad I found him." She needed to get his mind off of romance, but how? "So, you've been hitting the books really hard since the Combine. Are you ready for finals?"

"As ready as I'll ever be." He slid a hand under her t-shirt and rubbed her back. "The classes aren't difficult. I'm sure I'll do fine." He tilted his head and kissed her neck.

Leaning forward, she snatched the remote and pressed the power button. "I thought it would be fun to watch a movie. Let's see what's on. I can make some popcorn, too." Clicking the guide, she scrolled down the list—until Deke's lookalike placed a hand over hers, immediately halting her search.

So close she could feel his breath on her cheek, Deke whispered into her ear, "This is the first opportunity since I returned from Indianapolis we've had extended alone time." With his free hand, he rubbed his chin with his thumb and forefinger. "I want you, Elise."

Her inhale lodged in her throat as she fumbled for a reply. She couldn't afford to provide him even the slightest doubt of her complete devotion. Leaning into his embrace, she kissed his neck, then nibbled a trail to his ear. "And I want you." Completing the sentence in her mind only—*to go straight to hell and burn*. "It's just that I've planned this entire weekend, building up to the perfect denouement."

He drew back and tilted his head. "The perfect denouement, hmm. Interesting choice of words, but I can't imagine any better ending to this evening than making love."

"Come on, Deke. You've always humored me before. And how many times did you say you were glad we waited?" With any luck, her concocted comparison would give pause to Deke's clone. He might want her, but if he was as smart as he'd already proven, keeping in character would take precedence over immediate gratification. *Check, you son of a bitch.*

"Okay. We can watch a movie." He undressed her with his gaze. "But I won't promise beyond that. Lying next to you in bed tonight might take more restraint than I possess."

"Fair enough." She handed him the remote and stood. "You find a movie and I'll make popcorn." Thank God, she was able to at least buy some time.

She strode into the kitchen but, as she passed the farm table, she peered outside toward the spa. He had opened the top, and she saw his jeans draped over the edge of the canopy, she saw his jeans. She quietly opened the door.

"I thought you were going to make popcorn."

His voice froze her step, and she turned toward him. "I just noticed the top of the hot tub is open. It'll be too cool to use if I don't close it." She slipped outside, then seized his jeans and rummaged through a pocket for his keys.

"Let me get that cover."

Startled, she spun, his pants still in her hand. A hand flew to her chest. "Damn. You scared me."

He frowned. "You're a little jumpy. Maybe I should change the movie I chose. A horror flick might not be the best choice." He lowered the spa top, then tossed her an odd stare. "I'll take those."

She pinched her brows together. "Take what?"

"My jeans." He held out a hand.

Elise gazed at the pants in her hand, then held them out. "Sorry. You left them on the——"

"I know where I left them." He yanked them from her grasp and stepped aside. "After you."

Elise walked inside.

Deke-two followed, then closed the door. He hung his jeans over the stairway banister post and shot another stare toward Elise.

Feeling queasy at his abrupt response, she watched his demeanor. Did he suspect something? A surge of prickles stabbed through her body, then shot into her legs and arms. She'd been as nonchalant as she could muster, but his stare raised the hairs on the back of her neck. Whoever this man was, he possessed the skill and determination to pull off one helluva scheme. His intelligence and acting ability never faltered, but intuition told Elise he questioned her behavior. "You're so hot, Deke Madigan," she blurted out. Perhaps that would explain her momentary stare.

He smiled but said nothing.

"Popcorn. I'm on it." She stole into the kitchen, grabbed the popcorn, pot, and oil, mixed a batch, then covered it and set her concoction on the stove. When she opened a cabinet for a bowl, she peered around the corner.

Deke sat by the fireside, scrolling through the TV guide.

Whew. She dodged a bullet for the moment. But she still had to check his other pockets. If she couldn't find the truck key in his jeans, the only other option was his car. After filling the bowl, she returned to the great room and set the popcorn on the coffee table, then cuddled into the fake Deke. "What movie did you choose?"

"You'll see." He smirked and pressed Start.

Elise grabbed a handful of popcorn and tossed a few kernels into her mouth. She almost choked when the movie title, *Fatal Attraction,* appeared. Her body stiffened. His choice wasn't a coincidence. Elise now realized like a game of chess, every move this man made was intentional. He might not know how much she knew, but he definitely noticed her slight hesitation when she saw the movie he chose. If she wanted to free Deke, she needed to make her move now. She might not get another chance. She scooted forward. "Great choice, hon. Before it starts, I need to run to the restroom. Be back in a minute."

"Okay. Hurry."

She stood, kissed him on the cheek, then strode toward the stairway. Grabbing his jeans, Elise flew up the stairs, taking two steps at a time. She rushed through the master bedroom into the bathroom, then began searching his remaining pockets.

She heard him breathe before he spoke—and froze.

"Might you be searching for these?" He jingled the keys off the tip of a finger.

Chapter Nineteen

Daryl grabbed Elise's hair and twisted, yanking her head backward. "The question is, why?" He raised a brow. He knew her mannerisms. Did she really think she could fool him? He snarled. Pity. He really believed he could pull off the switch, but her body language had changed. She suspected something. How much, he wasn't sure—yet.

"Deke, what are you talking about?" She frowned, dropped the jeans on the floor, and twisted to face him, her head wrenched at an angle as she turned to see his face. "I don't understand what you're doing."

Jasper lunged forward and clenched his mouth around Daryl's wrist until he let go of Elise's hair.

"Jaz!" Screaming for the dog to follow her, she shot into the bedroom, pausing briefly beside the bed. "Let's go, Jaz." She flew downstairs and fumbled with the door. "Jaz. Come."

Growling, Jasper bared his teeth at Daryl, blocking him from following Elise.

"Go ahead, Elise. Run. But if you leave, you'll never see your dog again." Keeping Jasper's attention on his hands, Daryl swung a foot under the animal and knocked him off balance, then grabbed his collar and jerked him to the banister. "Take a look, Elise." He yanked the dog's collar until he yelped.

Struggling to free himself, Jaz pumped his legs, snarling and snapping his jaws as he attempted to bite Daryl.

But during his two-year preparation, Daryl had considered every possible scenario, including learning how to hold an angry dog at bay.

"Jaz." Elise peered around the door and gasped as she saw Jasper dangling from Daryl's outstretched hand, the dog's collar and a fistful of hair and flesh clenched in his grip.

He laughed with a toothy grin, pleased his training worked like a charm. "See? You leave, he dies. And don't think I'll hesitate a second before breaking his neck."

She entered the house and closed the door behind her. "Okay. I'm here. Now, let Jasper go."

"Not so fast, sweet pea." The dog's collar twisted in his hand as he slowly descended the stairs. "Have a seat, Elise." He hitched his chin toward the overstuffed chair in the great room.

She scowled and held her stance.

"That wasn't a suggestion. Sit." Again, he yanked the dog's collar until he yelped.

"Okay. Stop hurting Jaz." She edged sideways, her gaze locked with his, until she reached the chair, then sat. "Who are you?"

He chuckled. "I'm Deke Madigan, of course."

Again, she scowled. "I don't know who the hell you think you are, but you are definitely *not* Deke Madigan."

"Tsk, tsk, tsk. What a shame, Elise. I really had high hopes for us. I think I might have even given up other women for you, at least, for a while. But you ruined that, sweet pea."

"Don't call me that." She glared.

"But Deke used to call you sweet pea all the time."

"How do you know that? How do you know everything about Deke, and more importantly, why?" She leaned back into the chair, then pulled up her knees and wrapped her arms around them.

"Because he has the life I deserved. Now, it's my turn to ask a few questions. How did you know I wasn't Deke? I've watched him for years. I know everything, every little mannerism, pet names, the white roses. Tell me, what gave me away?"

"You must have tailed us, but you couldn't watch us everywhere." She shifted her gaze back and forth between the imposter and Jasper.

Leaning against the banister, he adjusted his grasp on the dog.

Jaz wriggled, twisting, and struggling to get free, but the grip on his neck held strong.

"No? Come on, Elise. I'd think, in your business, you'd at least be familiar with cameras, bugs, and basic surveillance equipment. I've watched Deke for two years, and when you came along, I simply added monitors and bugs to your condo and office."

"Why? I mean, who does that?" She shuddered, a disgusted expression pinching her facial features.

"You haven't answered my question yet. How did you know?"

"At first, I thought it was me. I convinced myself I was spooked by the murder."

"That was an accident. She saw me sneak out of your condo when I replaced a monitor. I couldn't let her ruin my plans."

Her eyes went wide, and she dropped her jaw. "You killed that woman?"

An icy sliver sliced down his back. Elise had just become a liability. He berated himself for slipping up and telling her he killed the woman in her condo complex. Could he kill Elise, too? Why did she have to be so curious? He glared at Elise, then cracked his neck to relieve the tension stiffening his shoulders. "I told you, it was an accident. And you still didn't answer my question." He straightened and jerked Jasper's collar again.

"Okay, okay. I guess I finally realized the only time I felt anxious was around you. Maybe you memorized everything about Deke, but you weren't Deke. Your kiss, your touch, your smell, I don't know. You just weren't my Deke, and you never could be."

Daryl felt his pulse throb in his neck. "Don't you dare judge me, Elise. I doubt you'd understand my circumstances even if I laid them in front of you. You've gotten everything you wanted in life from your rich daddy."

"Maybe. But Deke worked his ass off to earn a spot in the NFL. Do you really think you could step into his shoes? After a single practice, you'd be out on your ear." She huffed.

He harrumphed. "You little bitch. Do you think I'm an idiot? I've spent two years preparing for this challenge to prove myself worthy of whatever position Deke attained. With every sit-up, pushup, workout and run, I had my eye on the prize. I'm ready for whatever arises, and I figure, even if I miss the mark, once that contract is signed, I could feign an injury. A one-year contract would be plenty enough money to change my life for the better."

"And what about Deke? Do you plan on killing both of us?"

He lowered his gaze and scrunched Jasper's neck. "I never planned to kill anyone." Shifting his gaze to Elise, he flattened his lips. "I hoped you would find in me what Deke lacked. I treated you like a princess and gave you more attention than Deke ever did." He paused, hoping she would agree, reconsider, and realize his intent. "What I do with Deke depends entirely on him." Again, he waited for a reaction, but she didn't flinch. "You know he's still alive, don't you? How?"

"I don't know anything." She adjusted in her chair as if his very presence made her antsy.

He fisted his hands. Why did women always lie? "You're lying. That's why you wanted my keys. You wanted to sweep in and save him. And before you answer, you might want to consider Jasper. I don't like liars." He edged closer to Elise, still controlling Jasper by a hand gripping his collar.

"Okay. Yes. I found Deke in the truck."

"When?" He squinted, the fury inside him building to a crescendo.

"I ran across the truck cab searching for Jaz." Again, she adjusted her position.

"I'm not a cold-blooded murderer, Elise. You have no idea what motivated me to take such drastic measures. But sadly, you know far too much to let you go free."

"You don't have to kill me or Deke. Why don't you just lock me in the truck with him? Jaz, too."

"I built the compartment for only one guest, and a temporary one at that, darlin'." He tucked a strand of hair behind her ear. "Such a shame. I've actually grown quite fond of you. I'll miss you, but I don't believe for a second you'd keep my secret."

When Jasper suddenly squirmed and yanked free, he caught Daryl off guard.

Immediately, Daryl tried to compensate and lunged for the dog but only caught air.

Jaz darted outside through the rear door.

In one fluid moment, Daryl spun and gripped Elise's hair. He yanked downward until her head pressed tightly against the back of the chair. He sprang around and over her, clenched her wrists, then yanked her to a stand.

Before he had a chance to restrain Elise, a hand wrapped around his neck and swung him off the ground and onto his back. He snapped to his feet in a fluid ricochet and lunged forward with animal-like vengeance. Recognizing his opponent as Deke, he shoved his right shoulder into Deke's chest, then twisted and landed a vicious punch into his double's face.

Deke ducked quickly enough to escape the full force of Daryl's fist then, twisting, he delivered a haymaker into Daryl's stomach.

Stunned, Daryl's stare shot daggers. He was smarter and faster than Deke. It was high time to let his rival feel the impact of his vengeance. Anger seething, he drew back, and with the blood-curdling howl of a wild beast, he plowed forward into the brawl.

The savage attacks bled together with wildly swinging fists, blow-for-blow tearing into each other with equal ferocity, until a gunshot exploded through the night.

Deke halted.

Surprised, Daryl froze, his reactive stare locked on Elise.

She stood, legs spread, with arms locked firmly, the crosshairs of a revolver pointing directly at Daryl.

Before Deke could react, Daryl spun an arm around his neck. "Drop the gun, or I'll kill him."

She bit the corner of her lower lip but didn't flinch.

"You know I'll do it, Elise."

Deke jerked and twisted to break free, but Daryl's arm held fast. "Shoot him," he bellowed. "He killed Mr. Bailey."

"Mr. Bailey?" Elise glared at Daryl. "That sweet old man wouldn't hurt a flea. Why? Another accident?"

Daryl shrugged, then scowled. "Go ahead, Elise. Shoot, but before you do, you might be interested why I went to so much trouble to live my brother's life."

Elise's eyes went wide. "What are you talking about?"

"I don't have a brother," Deke bit out. "He's lying. Shoot, Elise."

Daryl laughed. "You know how I hate lies, Elise." He tightened his grip around Deke's neck. "Finding out I had an identical twin came as a surprise to me, too, brother dear. But the joke's on you. If you kill me, Elise, the secret my dear brother will never know dies with me."

Chapter Twenty

Stunned by the unfolding drama, Elise stood firm, her revolver aiming directly at the imposter's head.

From out of nowhere, Jasper leapt forward with open jaws and clenched Daryl's arm, ripping it from Deke's neck and hurling Daryl facedown onto the floor.

Deke planted a bare foot against his twin's neck to keep him from standing then, in one smooth motion, knelt over his back, pinning the man's shoulders to the ground. "Quick, Elise, I need a rope or something to tie his wrists."

She lowered the gun, stuffed the barrel into the back of her jeans, and sprinted into the kitchen. Heart racing, she rummaged through the drawers but found nothing resembling a rope. She darted into the laundry room.

"Hurry, Elise. He's bucking like a frickin' bronco. I can't hold him down much longer."

"Will an extension cord work?" she called out. Without waiting for an answer, she yanked the cord from a hook and dashed toward Deke.

"Perfect." He snatched the cord, then hog-tied the man's wrists to his ankles. "That should hold him."

"Dang, where did you learn how to do that, Deke?" Totally impressed with his skill, she'd never seen anyone hog-tie a criminal—not even on TV.

Standing, he wiped the sweat from his brow with his forearm. "We vacationed at a dude ranch when I was fourteen or fifteen, and they offered classes. I never thought I'd use the skill, but I had a crush on the girl teaching the session." He admired his handiwork for a beat, then turned toward Elise. "We make a great team, sweet pea."

The pet name sent a chill rippling down her arms, and she shuddered. "Would you mind changing that endearment to something else?" She hitched her chin toward the bound criminal. "Sweet pea was his favorite."

His eyes widened, then he narrowed his brows. "Seriously? How did he know that?"

"Apparently, he surveilled you for the last two years and added me when we met." She shook her head and shoved the man's shoulder with a foot. "Obsessed much?"

Deke clutched her arm and drew her into an embrace. "Well, he won't be watching us from a prison cell, and I'm pretty sure that's where he'll be spending the rest of his life." Let's give him one last image to remember us by." He kissed Elise long and hard.

The touch of his lips sent a ripple of heat throughout her entire body, and her toes curled.

She squeezed him so hard her breath caught in her throat. Kissing Deke made her realize why she felt so uneasy with the imposter. He might look like Deke, even act like Deke, but he definitely was not Deke. The difference was so evident in a mere kiss.

"For God's sake, get a room." Daryl snapped.

When Deke pulled away, he beamed a huge smile.

Finally, able to breathe, Elise trembled. She slid her hands down his arms.

"I've waited at least a month for that kiss. To be continued. But first—"

Biting on her lower lip, Elise stared. "How in the world did you escape that room in the truck?"

"I'll explain later." He shifted his gaze to his twin.

"There's only one way you could have escaped. You discovered the panic button." Daryl jerked his arms and legs, but the cord held firm. "I had a feeling that option was risky."

"Panic button?" She pinched her brows together.

"All right." Fingers splayed, he threw up his hands. "Before we start the barrage of questions, who are you?"

"Daryl." His glare shot daggers. "Daryl Quinn."

"So, Daryl Quinn, assuming you really are my twin, why not just approach me and introduce yourself? Why create this bizarre scheme?"

"Long story." He tugged against the electric cord binding him. "And it's a little hard to breathe like this, let alone talk."

"Suit yourself. Elise, is your phone handy?"

She scanned the room. Seeing her cell, she dashed toward the farm table and snatched the device. "As a matter of fact, yes." She walked toward Deke and opened the screen.

"Last chance, Daryl."

"Okay. Okay." Again, Daryl squirmed, but Deke's knots only tightened.

Deke leaned against the back of the sofa and rubbed his swollen cheek, then draped an arm around Elise. "I'm waiting."

"You'll call the police either way. Just get it over with."

"True. But don't you think I deserve to know the reason you stole my life?"

"You don't deserve anything from me. Your whole life has been a cake walk. Maybe I just wanted you to see what it's like to live in a one-room prison with no friends. At least I fed you."

"Right." Deke chuckled. "If you call peanut butter and honey sandwiches for a solid month food."

Daryl scowled. "Try eating them for the first eight years of your life."

Elise glared at Daryl. "If you're really Deke's twin, why doesn't he know anything about you?" What he did to her was nothing short of...of...what the hell could she call it? Emotional torture, molestation. Had the night gone the way she planned, could she tag the act as rape.

Deke squeezed her shoulder.

"For the same reason I didn't know about him until two years ago. No one told either of us." He huffed and slid his squinting gaze to Deke. "Did the people who raised you ever mention you were adopted?"

"As a matter of fact, they did." Deked crossed his legs. "But I didn't go all postal on them."

Daryl sneered. "Weren't you at least curious about your biological parents?"

"Of course. But my parents didn't know who they were, and the papers were held by a law firm and sealed until my twenty-first birthday."

"In case you hadn't noticed, you're twenty-two. I guess learning about your folks wasn't all that important." Daryl pushed at the floor to rearrange his position but, for all his efforts, the adjustment did little to help. He snarled.

Deke drew in a long breath, then blew the air out. "In case you didn't notice, I've been really tied up, what with college and earning a spot in the NFL. I planned to do a search once I secured my future."

"Don't bother. Your mother died—two years ago."

A stab of sorrow pierced Elise's heart and she gasped. "Oh, God, Deke. I'm so sorry."

His jaw jutted forward. "Are you freakin' kidding me? Why the hell are you sorry for him? He didn't even know her or care enough to search. I grew up with her."

"I'd say that makes you the lucky twin, not me." Deke's body went rigid. "I'll never have an opportunity to know her."

Lowering her gaze, Elise thought of how awful her childhood might have been without her parents. She shifted her gaze to Daryl. "I'm sure losing your mother devastated you."

Again, Daryl huffed. "Like you care." He angled his head to see Deke. "And you. You didn't have to grow up in the back room of bars, eating scraps, watching drunk men fondling your mother, or molesting women only a few feet away. And you didn't have to watch your momma cry herself to sleep more times than not or take care of her when she wasted away to nothing from cancer. I quit school, tried to make enough money to pay for treatments, but there was never enough."

Elise bit her lower lip, envisioning Daryl's description, and she couldn't help but feel sorry for him. "That's awful, Daryl. I'm so sorry that happened. But none of that was Deke's fault. Why punish him?"

Deke pushed off the sofa and walked toward the rear entrance, then stared outside for a long, silent beat before turning toward Daryl. "How did we get separated in the first place? And where was our father?"

"Now, he cares," Daryl bit out.

"Those are two good questions, Daryl. And please, answer mine." Elise stooped down to face him. "Why do you blame Deke for any of this? He had no idea you existed. You've known about him for two years." As much as Daryl had done to

Deke—and her—she could see how much he held inside. Of course, that was no excuse for his actions—especially if he killed two people. She leaned back onto her calves. "Did your mother tell you how you and Deke got separated?"

"Yeah. On her deathbed." Daryl detailed their mother's background, how she was about to graduate med school when a group of football players gang-raped her at a party. How her parents disowned her when she told them she was pregnant and decided to keep her child. And how she walked away and tried to raise twins on her own but couldn't afford both boys. "Even though we lived in government housing most of my childhood, I worked hard in school. Momma promised that was how to earn a good living. I believed one day I'd make enough money to take care of her for the rest of her life, but cancer didn't get the memo. It had another agenda. Cancer robbed both of our lives. I couldn't go to college because I needed to take care of her. And when she died, I swore I'd find the guys who raped her and make them all pay for destroying her life."

Deke sat on the sofa and lowered his head to his hands.

Elise wrinkled her forehead. "I get you had a rough childhood, but that doesn't explain why you chose to punish Deke."

"Momma wouldn't tell me the names of the men who attacked her or why she chose to keep me instead of Deke, but she told me how proud she was of both of us and how to find him. When I saw what a cushy life he had while we struggled every day, I guess I just snapped."

Resting his arms on his knees, Deke shifted his gaze to meet Daryl's. "I think I can shed some light on why our mother made the choice she did. There's a part of your story you aren't aware of."

This time, Elise laid a hand on Deke's shoulder. She had no idea what he knew, but his pinched expression shot a wave of anxiety swirling down her back. She suspected whatever puzzle piece Deke slid into place would change all their lives.

Chapter Twenty-One

Steepling his forefingers, Deke continued, "You said our mother never told you why she chose to keep you, right?"

Daryl nodded. "I'll never be sorry for growing up with her, but just seeing your cushy life sparked a fire in the pit of my stomach. That kind of money could have saved her life."

"Are you interested in why she gave me away?" Childhood memories flooded his thoughts.

"Don't bother. Nothing you can say would change anything. You were chosen to live a cushy life and I was dealt a life of hard knocks. So what?"

"Hear me out, Daryl." He paused, hoping to spark his twin's interest. He saw only a bitterly broken man. "My parents had a good life, but more than anything, they wanted children. When my mother discovered she could never conceive, her heart broke. But an old friend of theirs, Doctor Wilson—"

"Your folks knew the doc?" He snapped a gaze toward Deke.

"Yes. Doctor Wilson told them of a young woman who had a very sick baby. She couldn't afford the years of treatments that lay ahead. Treatments his prognosis dictated necessary to save her child's life. She agreed to let my parents adopt her boy if they promised to provide him with the best medical care available, which would likely continue throughout his life. That baby was me, Daryl."

Daryl frowned. "You're lying. You're an athlete. You had to have played ball since you were a kid."

"I'm not lying." Deke slipped off his t-shirt and pointed to a zipper-like disfigurement barely visible beneath his chest hair. "See this scar?"

Daryl nodded.

"I was born with CHD—Congenital Heart Disease—and had several surgeries before I was a year old. Without those surgeries, I would have died."

Elise stared, wide-eyed. "I never noticed that scar. Why didn't you tell me? Is it dangerous for you to play ball? I mean, what would happen if you were tackled and—"

"I'm fine, Elise. My scar isn't as noticeable now that I have hair on my chest, but when I was a kid, I was really self-conscious. My parents finally convinced me the wound was a battle scar." He chuckled. "And I was lucky, Daryl. All my life, my parents encouraged me to eat well and exercise to make my heart strong. They put in a swimming pool and playground for my workouts. Eventually, I got to the point I actually enjoyed working out. I guess that's why I chose to be an athlete. By the time I was in my teens, I could outrun anyone my age and could throw a football farther than most. My parents still worried about other kids tackling me. They wouldn't let me join a team until high school, and even then, my coach watched out for me. I played quarterback, so that worked out pretty well. As long as my team protected me, I was good."

Elise hugged him. "That explains a lot, but what about college and pro ball? You can't just tell the other teams to avoid sacking you."

"My doctor says I'm no more at risk now than anyone else."

She turned to Daryl. "It looks like your mother didn't randomly choose to give Deke a cushy life. She gave him up to save his life. That must have killed her. But she was so lucky to have you." Elise flashed an adoring gaze toward Deke, then returned to Daryl. "You have to admit, Deke's childhood was pretty tough, too."

"Yeah." Daryl went limp, as if the toxic energy feeding his vengeance drained. Cheek against the floor, he closed his eyes for a long moment. "I'm sorry, Deke. I didn't know."

"Neither did I." He stood and approached Daryl. Placing a hand on his arm, he gently squeezed. "Damn. You got some guns there. No wonder my body is still throbbing from your punches. Hey, I hope you'll tell me all about our mother sometime. It sounds like she was a very strong woman."

Daryl nodded.

"But you realize we still have to call the police, right?"

Again, Daryl nodded. "What I did was really f-ed up. The anger seething inside me fed on itself, and with no one to blame for Momma's death. It consumed me." He turned to Elise. "For the record, I didn't kill Mr. Bailey. He came across my truck parked on your property. I tried to tell him I would move, but I admit, I got a little huffy when he acted like a hard ass, saying he'd call the cops. He refused to give me a break. I shoved him and probably scared him. He backed away several steps, then his hand flew to his chest, and he collapsed. I swear, I didn't try to hurt the old man. When he didn't get up, I leaned over him. I thought he must have hit his head on a rock. I felt his neck for a pulse, but his empty stare looked just like Momma's when she died."

Elise's fists flew to her waist. "Do you really expect me to believe you after you confessed to killing my neighbor?"

Deke's eyes went wide. "You killed a woman at Elise's condo?"

"Yes." He lowered his gaze. "I'm not proud of what I did, but her death is all on me. I panicked. I didn't intend to kill her. I just wanted to stop her from telling anyone what she saw." He stretched his neck to look straight into Elise's eyes. "I don't blame you for not believing me. I wouldn't believe me, either. I swear to you, though, I'm telling the truth about the old man. Have the medical examiner do an autopsy on your Mr. Bailey. That would prove I'm not lying."

Deke watched the change in his brother's face and demeanor as the fight in Daryl dissolved.

Elise bit on her bottom lip. "'We grow accustomed to the dark when the light is cut away.'"

What? Deke snapped a confused gaze to Elise. "Where did that come from?"

"A quote by Emily Dickinson I remember from my college psych classes." Her gaze slid from Daryl to Deke. "I'm no psychologist, but as Daryl explained his actions, he reminded me of some case studies. When his mother died, Daryl's life caved in on him. Surrounded by darkness with no one to light his way, his mind compensated and rationalized his behavior."

"I wouldn't blame you if you left me to rot in jail."

Deke softened the tension in his face. "You have family, now." Kneeling, he untied the cord from Daryl's ankles, leaving his wrists knotted behind his back. Then he helped his brother stand. "What do you say we take this one day at a time? If you're willing to confess, Elise and I will drive you to the Forsyth County Police station. A confession has to help your case."

She pursed her lips, then added, "You'll need counseling to help you recover from your trauma. And you'll likely have jail time for killing my neighbor."

"I'm glad my mother died believing in me. What went down would have broken her heart. She was a strong woman, Deke, and a good mother."

""You can do this, Daryl. Use your time in jail to get your head straight and turn your life around. And I'll visit. I promise." He draped an arm around Elise and drew her close, then kissed the top of her head.

Gazing upward, she smiled and stared at his piercing blue eyes. "He's right, Daryl. This isn't the end. It's a new beginning." Elise marveled at the conviction and sincerity in Deke's tone. He truly felt compassion for his brother, despite Daryl's obsession to take over his life.

From the moment Deke touched her shoulder that afternoon after the Georgia-Carolina game, he'd enchanted her. Not his appearance...not his personality...or the future she knew he'd procure in the NFL. Deke possessed an intangible essence like no man she'd ever known, and no one—not even his identical twin—could ever duplicate his soul. As much as Elise had tried to convince herself to the contrary, her heart always knew a spark was missing in her life, until she met Deke.

From his perch at the top of the stairs, Jasper barked, then scuttled down the steps and nuzzled his way between Elise and Deke, then sat, tail wagging.

She chuckled. "I think Jaz approves." Cuddling into the crook beneath Deke's shoulder, she wrapped her arms around his waist and squeezed.

Epilogue

Seven months later...

Elise leaned back against the Adirondack loveseat and stared at the starlit sky. "What a beautiful night."

"I can't believe how many stars you can see here. No city lights in the background or pollution to muddy the sky. I completely understand why you two moved here." Britt turned toward Elise. "I'm glad the Daryl affair didn't taint your decision."

"Please, Britt, my wife's run-in with my long-lost brother was not an affair."

In the middle of a long swig of cola, Matt leaned forward and spewed out a mouthful with a boisterous laugh. "Poor choice of words, Britt." He shifted his gaze. "Speaking of your brother, how's he doing, Deke?"

"Better. You guys know Mr. Bailey's autopsy showed no evidence of foul play. He died of a massive heart attack." Deke raked his fingers through his hair. "But Deke raked his fingers through his hair. "But Daryl?"

Elise leaned forward and placed a hand over Deke's knee. "He still feels guilty he didn't reach out to his biological parents when he turned twenty-one."

"Come on, man. You had no idea what was going on." Matt kicked at Deke's shoe.

"I know." Deke nodded. "But I can't help thinking I could have made a difference, maybe saved that woman's life."

"You're making a difference now, Deke." Britt rested her elbows on her knees and stared into the blazing fire swirling upward into the night sky.

Deke nodded. Leaning back, he stretched an arm around Elise's shoulder. "That's what Daryl says, too. His mental instability kept him from being held criminally responsible for Carla Attwood's homicide—Elise's neighbor. The Georgia Central State Psychiatric Hospital in Milledgeville is helping him come to terms with what he did. Elise and I visit him quite a bit, and we're encouraged by his progress."

"We're hoping he'll be awarded an unsupervised visit for the holidays," Elise added. "And if he continues to improve, the court will consider vacating the remanded program at Milledgeville to time spent, or the minimum required." A long silence ensued. She lowered her gaze, mesmerized by the flickering fire.

Britt took a sip from her glass of Merlot. "Hey, Matt, why is it you and Deke decided to pass on alcohol when all of your teammates constantly party?"

Elise shot a sideways glance toward Deke. She'd never thought to mention a word to Britt, but she found the question interesting. Palms forward and brows high, she raised both hands and shrugged.

Matt chuckled. "Let's just say his Papaw convinced us to lay off booze before we acquired a taste for the stuff."

Elise snickered and watched as the fire's glow cast shadows across her friends' faces.

"Aside from the craziness last March, and your hectic schedule, not to mention the stress of your beautiful wedding, you two look happier than I've ever seen you," Britt mused. "And why not? I can't get enough of this view."

The full moon reflected off the glass-like surface of Lake Lanier and the velvety, star-studded night greeted the treetops. "I can't imagine anywhere I'd rather be." Elise echoed. She cuddled into the crook of her husband's arm. Her husband, she still wasn't used to the concept, but after everything she and Deke went through in March, they knew a future together was etched in stone.

They moved into the lake house in May and planned a September wedding, inviting only intimate friends and family. As a little girl, Elise had envisioned marrying her Prince Charming in the back yard of the lake house with the spectacular view of the water as a backdrop. Her childhood dream came true, and the evening wedding couldn't have been more beautiful. Her father walked her down the aisle, and she finally had the chance to wear her gorgeous white gown with the ice-blue trim. Never would she forget the look on Deke's face as he took her hand.

"Wow. You're more stunning than I've ever seen you, Elise," he'd whispered. "Are you ready to become my wife?"

She'd smiled and nodded.

As they said their vows, the sunset cast a brilliant, peach-colored hue across the landscape, as if God's grace shone over their union.

Jasper climbed onto the Adirondack loveseat and plopped between Deke and Elise.

She smiled as her thoughts returned to the present.

"Hey, boy." Deke tugged Jaz onto his lap and closed the gap between he and Elise. "Sorry, buddy. You have to share her, now." Returning his arm to rest over her shoulders, he drew her close.

She raised her gaze to meet his. The fire flicker reflected in his eyes. Completely content, she snuggled against his warm chest and stared at the starlit night.

"I love you so much, Elise," he whispered softly.

His warm breath on her neck shot a quiver of delight through her entire body.

Crooking a finger under her chin, he gently turned her head, then pressed his lips over hers.

A shiver ran down her back all the way to her toes—and she giggled as she felt them slightly curl. "I'll love you forever, Deke."

~ *The End* ~

About the Author

USA Today & Amazon Best Selling Author, Casi McLean, pens novels to stir the soul with romance, suspense, and a sprinkle of magic. Her writing crosses genres from ethereal, captivating shorts with eerie twist endings, to believable time slips, mystical plots, and sensual romantic suspense.

Known for enchanting stories with magical description, McLean entices readers with fascinating hooks to hold them captive in storylines they can't put down. Her romance entwines strong, believable heroines with delicious, hot heroes to tempt the deepest desires, then fans the flames, sweeping readers into their innermost romantic fantasies.

With suspenseful settings and lovable characters, you'll devour, you'll see, hear, and feel the magical eeriness of one fateful night. You'll swear time travel could happen, be mystified by other worldly images, and feel the heat of romantic suspense, but most of all you'll want more.

Casi's latest series enters the realm of political thrillers with Reign Of Fire, exclusively found in the #1 bestselling, romantic suspense boxset, Love Under Fire. Watch the trailer exclusively on this page.

Inspired by freak accidents, strange phenomena, and eerie lore attached to Atlanta's man-made Lake Sidney Lanier, USA Today Best-Selling Author, Casi McLean spins a spine-chilling time-travel, romantic suspense series in her Lake Lanier Mysteries.

What if excavation created more than a lake? What if explosions triggered a seismic shift, creating a portal that connected past to future?

Beneath The Lake, Lake Lanier Mysteries Book #1 won 2016 Best Romantic Suspense and the Gayle Wilson Award of Excellence. Watch the trailer.

Beyond The Mist, book #2 in her romantic time slip treasure chest, is a stunning tribute to the victims and first responders of the 911 World Trade Center terrorist attack. Watch the trailer.

Between The Shadows brings the saga full circle with an amazing time slip to 1865 and a search for the Confederate gold. Don't miss this trailer.

SIGN UP for Casi McLean's Newsletter and receive a FREE Story!
Be first to find out about all my New Releases including the next story from my Deep State Mysteries!

Watch all Casi's trailers and follow her on her YouTube Channel.

And follow Casi on these sites:

Amazon
Website
BookBub
Twitter
Facebook
Instagram

A Note to the Reader

A personal request:

If you enjoyed this story, please post a review. Reviews are the lifeblood of an author's world, and they mean so much not only to inspire my new stories, but also to boost my career by letting other readers know my stories are worth reading. From the bottom of my heart, thank you for your support!

Warmest Regards,

Casi McLean

Please post a review on these sites:

Amazon
BookBub
Goodreads

More Books by Casi McLean

Destiny
Five Novelettes With A Twist

Destiny

The Gift

After Midnight

Convergent

The Pegasus Chronicle

Deep State Mysteries

Rein of Fire

The List: Alyssa's Revenge

Lake Lanier Mysteries

A Time Travel Romantic Suspense Series

Beneath the Lake

Beyond The Mist

Between the Shadows

Lake Lanier Mysteries

To give you a sneak peek of my stories, I've included book descriptions and excerpts for you. Enjoy.

Beneath the Lake Won 2019 PRG Best Time Travel Novel

2016 Best Romantic Suspense

Gayle Wilson Award of Excellence

The story was inspired by the freak accidents, strange phenomena, and eerie lore attached to Atlanta's man-made Lake Sidney Lanier.

But what if the excavation created more than a lake? What if explosions triggered a seismic shift that created a portal connecting past to future? Lake Lanier Mysteries evolved from that premise.

Time Travel, Mystery, Thriller, Romantic Suspense with Supernatural Elements.

Beneath The Lake

Book 1—Lake Lanier Mysteries

Print and Audible Versions Available

A ghost town, buried beneath Atlanta's famous man-made Lake Lanier, reportedly lures victims into a watery grave. But when Lacey Montgomery's car spins out of control and hurtles into the depths of the icy water, she awakens in the arms of a stranger, in a town she's never heard of––34 years *before* she was born.

When the 2012 lawyer tangles with a 1949 hunk, fire and ice swirl into a stream of sweltering desire. Bobby Reynolds is smitten the moment the storm-ravaged woman opens her eyes and, despite adamant protest, Lacey falls in love with a town destined for extinction, and the man who vows to save his legacy.

Threatened by a nefarious stalker, the wrath of bootleggers, and twists of fate, Lacey must find the key to a mysterious portal before time rips the lovers apart, leaving their star-crossed spirits to wander forever through a ghost town buried beneath the lake.

Excerpt

Chapter 1

Lake Lanier, Georgia—June 2011

A final thud hurled him backward, flailing through brush and thickets like a rag doll. Grasping at anything to break momentum, Rob's hand clung to a branch wedged into the face of the precipice. Spiny splinters sliced his skin. Blood oozed and trickled into his palms, and one by one, his fingers slowly slipped.

A sharp crack echoed through the silence of the ravine as the bough succumbed to his weight. He plummeted into free-fall. Clenching his eyes, he drew in a deep breath, terrified of the pain, the mauling that waited on the jagged rocks below.

When icy water broke his fall, the chill kept him from losing consciousness. He spun, straining to see, but darkness enveloped him. Soggy clothing pulled him deeper—deeper into the murky, fathomless depths. He wrestled to squirm free from the waterlogged jacket dragging him down to a watery grave, watched the coat disappear into black obscurity. Panic gripped his stomach, or was it death that snaked around his chest, squeezing, squeezing, squeezing the air, the life from his body? Lack of oxygen burned his lungs, beckoning surrender, and a shard of rage pierced his gut as reality set in. He lunged upward with one last thrust and burst from the water's deadly grip, gasping for air. A gurgling howl spewed from the depths of his soul and echoed into silence.

Sunlight shimmered across a smooth, indigo lake, but aside from the slight ripples of his own paddling, nothing but stillness surrounded him. He floated toward the shore, sucking deep breaths into his lungs until the pummeling in his chest subsided. When he reached the water's edge, he hoisted his body onto the soft red clay and collapsed while the sun's warmth drained the tension from his body.

No one knew he had survived. The rules had shifted. Now he could reinvent himself, become a stealth predator. His target: Lacey Madison Montgomery.

Beyond The Mist

Book 2—Lake Lanier Mysteries

Print and Audible Versions Available

When a treacherous storm spirals Piper Taylor into the arms of Nick Cramer, an intriguing lawyer, she never expected to fall in love. But when he disappears, she risks her life to find him; unaware the search would thrust her into international espionage, terrorism, and the space-time continuum.

Nick leads a charmed life except when it comes to his heart. Haunted by a past relationship, he can't move forward with Piper despite the feelings she evokes. When he stumbles upon a secret portal hidden beneath Atlanta's Lake Lanier, he seizes the chance to correct his mistakes.

A slip through time has consequences beyond their wildest dreams. Can Piper find Nick and bring him home before he alters the fabric of time, or will the lovers drift forever *Beyond The Mist?*

Excerpt

Chapter 1

Lake Lanier, GA June 2012

A soft mist hovered over the moonlit lake, beckoning, luring him forward with the seductive enticement of a mermaid's song. The rhythmic clatter of a distant train moaned in harmony with a symphony of cricket chirps and croaking frogs. Mesmerized, Nick Cramer took a long breath and waded deeper into the murky cove. Dank air, laden with a scent of soggy earth and pine crawled across his bare arms. The hairs on the back of his neck bristled, shooting a prickle slithering around his spine into an icy pool quivering in the pit of his abdomen. Shots of fiery energy electrified his senses, thousands of needles spewed venom into his chest until his stomach heaved and rancid bile choked into his throat. He clenched his fingers into a tight fist, determined to fight through the fear now consuming him.

I can do this—he forged ahead—*only a few more steps and*—a sudden surge swirled around him, yanking him into a whirling vortex; a violent blue haze dragged him deeper, deeper beneath the lake into the shadowy depths. Heart pounding, he battled against the force, twisting, pulling back toward the surface with all his strength but, despite his muscular build, he spun like a feather in the wind into oblivion. When the mist dissolved, Nick Cramer had vanished.

Between The Shadows

Book 3—Lake Lanier Mysteries

Print and Audible Versions Available

Thrust back in time, Kenzi never expected to confront deadly villains—let alone fall in love with one.

After her friend, York, encounters the ghostly image of a young woman, Mackenzie Reynolds seizes the opportunity to initiate a time jump, thrusting them back to 1865 Georgia. Resolved to thwart the girl's untimely fate, Kenzi stumbles into a deadly conflict over a stockpile of stolen Confederate gold.

An injured Civil War survivor, James Adams departs for home with a war-fatigued companion he's determined to help. After pilfering a horse and kidnapping a woman, he never dreamed his hostage would steal his heart.

Kenzi and James must unravel a deadly plot, while helping York save his ghost woman from a brutal death. But can she leave York in a violent past to save James's life?

Excerpt

"Don't you dare die on me, James Adams."

Kenzi pressed a wad of blood-soaked gauze against his abdomen. "I won't lose you. Not now."

Barely clinging to life, the man opened his eyes a slit, raised the gun still tightly gripped in his hand and shot off a round.

Stunned, she snapped around. "No." Screaming, she dove for the barrel through a hazy blue mist.

Again, the gun rang out as the patient fell unconscious.

"Help. Someone, please help".

A muted voice murmured from beyond the fog. "Dr. Reynolds? Is that you?"

Her frantic reply cried out, "Yes, of course it's me. Hurry. He's bleeding out."

"Brady..." James's voice faded as he slipped into semiconscious mumbling.

Yanking the pistol from his grip with her right hand, she maintained pressure with her left. A heartbeat later, the cylinder encasing them rotated open. Kenzi stood then sprinted across the room past an attendant then pounded on a fist-sized alert button affixed to the wall. The resulting alarm shrieked through the underground chamber, reverberating as it radiated throughout the compound. A second man dressed in a white jumpsuit burst through double doors.

"Gurney. Now." Kenzi screamed at both attendants. "And O-Neg blood. Hurry. Go, go, go." She ran to James and knelt beside him. Lifting his head, she slid a knee underneath it for support and smoothed a chunk of his dark brown hair from his face. "I've sacrificed way too much to have you die now," she whispered. "My ass will burn for this. Not to mention the repercussions for abandoning York."

Pulse racing, she checked his bandage. Despite her efforts, streams of crimson still oozed from the wound. Pressing again on the gauze, she shook her head. "Oh God. I have no idea what blood type you are, but you should tolerate O-negative." She pressed harder on his wound. "Jesus help you, James. You've lost so much blood. Just please, hang on."

Again, the double doors swung wide. This time, a gurney pushed through, followed by the two men. One ran to Kenzi's side.

"Help me lift him." Her hands, slick with blood, shot to her white T-top, already drenched in crimson. On a second thought, she swept them down the rear of her jeans. Then, sliding her slippery arms beneath his back, she braced her stance with one bent knee.

"One, two, three." They heaved him in tandem onto the gurney. She snatched a bottle of Betadine from the attached supply basket and doused her hands then splashed more on James's forearm, grasped an IV and punctured a vein on the inside of his wrist with the sterile needle. Once connected, she hooked the blood pouch on the IV pole and barked at the team, "Let's move. If this man bleeds out, there will be hell to pay."

The men, poised with hands on the side of the rails, awaited their next move. "Where to, Dr. Reynolds?"

Kenzi stared at James's ashen face, worried her meager experience wasn't enough to save his life—but she had no option. "Surgery."

Springing into action, one man rolled the gurney down the hallway, while a second leapt onto the base and slipped an oxygen mask over James's nose and mouth. "I hope this guy isn't allergic to Propofol." He attached an anesthesia drip to the IV. "Judas Priest. What happened to him to cause such a gaping wound?" "He was shot...with a musket

Deep State Mysteries

Reign of Fire
Book 1—Deep State Mysteries

Print and Audible Versions Available

To expose a faction threatening America's democracy, Emily Rose joins forces with a team investigating her sister's murder, but she never expects to fall in love—or to encounter her twin's ghost.

Ashton Frasier accepts his detective career choice means a life of bachelorhood—until Emily Rose blows into his world.

Surrounded by danger with the country's democracy at stake, Emily and Ash must protect the White House while taming their mysterious burning passion—lit by cunning spirit with good intentions.

Can a ghost spark love in the midst of chaos?

Excerpt

Chapter One

Alyssa Rose shifted her gaze in every direction, searching for suspicious bystanders. Her cloak-and-dagger cover had her exit the Capitol through the door next to the ladies' room. The out-of-character detour might have been an insignificant detail, but evading possible surveillance made her breathe easier. Walking east of the Capitol altered her routine, so a side trip to this particular mail drop provided a prime spot to send her letter under the radar.

Trembling as she approached her destination, she scrutinized everyone, zeroing in on their eyes. If she observed someone with a shifty gaze or noticed an unusual glance in her direction, she'd walk past the postal box and circle back later. No one could see her mail this letter.

Taking a deep breath, she slid the envelope from beneath her coat, ran her finger across the address then quickly slipped the letter into the mailbox at the corner of Independence and Pennsylvania. A cold chill slithered around her neck, shooting pins and needles in every direction before tightening the knot already twisting in her stomach. Drawing together the lapels of her royal-blue coat, she snatched the soft cashmere and cast one more glance around before striding across Pennsylvania toward 2nd Street.

The icy tingle numbing Alyssa to the bone had little to do with the cool March weather. The crisp air might have exacerbated the sensation, but her accidental discovery initiated the anxiety, and she couldn't erase the images seared into her mind. If anyone discovered what she saw, her very life would be in jeopardy. God, she wished she could un-know what now dominated her thoughts.

Only a few weeks ago, Alyssa lived a blissful life of naiveté. Her family reared her to hold dear the advantages her country bestowed, and when her senior field trip took the class to Williamsburg, Virginia, she experienced a strong sense of patriotism that continued to blossom.

Wyatt, her brother, fanned the fire blazing in her belly. Despite his horrendous accident in Afghanistan, his love for country burned eternal. If anything, the explosion that took his legs fanned the flames, and he encouraged Alyssa to use her skills to fight for a better country from within the body that created the laws. An intern job would help her learn policy to springboard to a political profession and open doors where she could make a real difference.

She worked her butt off long and hard to secure a spot in this program. A budding Intern for Congressman Derek Winfield, Alyssa saw this job as her big chance. Granted, the position seemed mundane, if not ridiculous. She simply walked in, picked up a pile of messages and dispersed them to offices on The Hill accordingly.

Email would have been a lot easier and faster. At first, she thought the task was a newbie-only job assigned to interns, forcing them to learn the lay of the land. But Derek explained email messages were traceable. They were etched into hard drives and nearly impossible to erase.

So, for the time being interoffice mail delivery was her job and a rung of the ladder she'd be happy to pass on when the time came. Until then, she didn't mind starting her career at the bottom rung of the ladder. The mailroom had its perks. Playing courier allowed her to walk historic streets and take in the ambiance, imagining the town during different eras and all the presidents who once strolled on antiquated roads beneath her.

Her innocent walks around Capitol Hill mingled business with pleasure. Ear buds firmly tucked in place, she listened to her favorite mix, while chalking up her health goal of ten thousand-steps. The bustle between L'Enfant Plaza and the Capitol energized her. Wide-eyed, she relished the inspiration America's forefathers instilled—until the dreadful day an arbitrary Starbucks patron collided with her as he bolted into the store. Memories swirling, her mind replayed the fateful day in a 24/7 constant loop. How could such an innocent random event spiral into this very real nightmare?

Purse slung over her shoulder, with a tray of coffee orders in one hand and a stack of to-be-delivered messages in the other, Alyssa had no control as her balancing act flew into the air, leaving a deluge of coffee-splattered, mocha-scented letters cluttering the entrance. "No, no, no." After flinging her hands, she snatched a pile of napkins and frowned at the mess surrounding her. She drew in a deep breath. Indignation seething inside, she clenched a fist to repress her reaction to a simmer.

"Son of a bitch." The dark-haired man's attention dropped to his camelhair coat. Brushing off coffee beads to keep them from soaking into his lapel, he flashed a gaze toward Alyssa, offering a lame apology. "Sorry. This mess is totally on me."

A tinge of satisfaction befell her, as she eyed his splattered attire. "I can see that." She chuckled.

He followed her line of vision and glanced downward. "Perfect." Grabbing more napkins, he cleaned whipped cream from his shoes then wiped his pants before noticing a sizable blotch on the pocket of his camelhair. "Damn it." Tugging off the coat, he draped it across the side of the condiment stand and reached for an arbitrary towel clumped into a mound beside him, then pressed on the stain. Not until he appeared to be satisfied with his own results, did he return his attention to Alyssa, now squatting beside him, cleaning the coffee puddle. "Here, let me help you."

She rolled her eyes but said nothing, although her thoughts rebuked him. *It's about damn time you focused on the chaos you caused...*

The stranger knelt with towel in hand and sloshed it around in the pool of coffee, making the mess exponentially worse, while Alyssa fought to keep her boiling frustration at bay. Shifting her gaze to her scattered and smothered envelopes, she turned and duck-walked, gathering them into a drenched pile. She clenched her jaw, then shook and examined each packet, an effort that did little more to minimize the damage than changing splotches to dribbles.

When an attendant came to the rescue and began mopping the floor, the stranger stood, retrieved his coat, and draped it over an arm. "Damn. Can this day get any worse?" He glanced at his watch. "Son of a—now, I'm running late." Turning toward Alyssa, he reached into his back pocket and drew out a business card then handed it to her. "Take this. I'll pay your dry-cleaning bill. Just shoot me an email." Instead of buying a coffee, he smacked open the door and rushed outside, quickly disappearing into the busy crowd.

Alyssa's last nerve had her grinding her teeth as she inspected her own coat for stains. Surprised her clothing escaped the coffee cascade, she stuffed the man's proffer into her pocket without even glancing at his name. She felt a bit atoned that the bulk of the mess splashed over him as opposed to her. But a quick glance at her letters doused the brief restitution. Again, she blotted the notes in her charge in an attempt to salvage them, hoping the incident wouldn't cost her job.

When the attendant finished mopping the floor, he asked if he could remake her order.

Alyssa nodded and thanked him, still wiping her mess. Why did the collision have to happen to her? She cussed the arrogant man under her breath. How dare he blow her off after causing the incident?

Instead of the attendant, a manager returned to the scene with a carryout tray of fresh coffee. "This batch is on the house. I saw that whole scenario go down." He shook his head. "That guy could have at least helped you with your mail, since he was the reason your envelopes were soiled."

"Thank you so much." Alyssa appreciatively took the order. "I'm sorry to make such a mess."

The manager shrugged. "Hey, you did nothing wrong. No worries. Stuff happens."

"Tell that to my boss." Rolling her eyes, Alyssa splayed the pile of notes in her hand. "How can I deliver these to senators and congressmen?" Heat raged in her cheeks. She squeezed her eyes shut for a long beat, resisting the march of berating anger clenching her stomach. True, the accident wasn't her fault, but if she hadn't been so engrossed in listening to her music, she might have seen the man busting through the door and avoided the mishap altogether.

The manager smiled and raised an eyebrow. "The damage looks superficial. Maybe you could just replace the envelopes?" He gazed at the soggy array. "Look, the coffee didn't stain the addresses beyond recognition, and I doubt the damage seeped through to the inside messages."

"Perhaps…" Alyssa's frown faded as she inspected the notes and considered his idea. "You might be right. Thanks." If she hurried to her office and simply switched the envelopes, she could deliver the messages with only a slight delay…no one would be the wiser. Gathering her paperwork and coffee, she rushed outside then scurried to her office, assured the plan just might save her ass.

In theory, the switch was a no-brainer. She never dreamed one instinctual *cover-your-ass* choice could threaten her life. Opening the coffee-stained envelopes and switching the notes to identical, deliverable packets seemed the perfect solution—until she discovered the one note never intended for delivery…the note that validated the existence of a shadow government.

Geez, if only she hadn't opened that wretched letter. She gasped the moment she saw an immediate burn order splashed in red across the top of the page above a simple title: The List. As she read on, she swallowed hard, her breath catching in her throat. She had no idea how deep the faction went, or which treasonous federal officials would be revealed once the list was decoded.

Racking her brain, she couldn't recall where the delivery had come from. She couldn't remember picking it up from any of the offices. But she had to admit her mindless deliveries rarely demanded her undivided attention. Still, the envelope was smaller than the others, and it didn't carry the standard Federal Government insignia.

A loud honking from a car speeding through the traffic signal brought her thoughts back to the moment. *Dear God*. The last thing she needed was a jolt to boost her adrenaline.

Biting the edge of her bottom lip, Alyssa shoved her trembling hands into her pockets and picked up her pace, rationalizing her decision. She didn't intend to snoop that day. She simply couldn't deliver soggy, damaged mail and expect no one would notice. An entry-level job meant no demotions existed. If she didn't perform up to expectations, firing was the only alternative. Her priority…she had to save her dream-job.

Slowing her pace, she entered the Capitol Rotunda and gazed at the vast marvel surrounding her. How did her dream morph into the nightmare now clenching her throat in a stranglehold…a nightmare from which she couldn't awaken? She shuddered. Not in her wildest dreams had she ever expected the politicized bureaucrats and pundits on Capitol Hill would swallow her whole.

Discovering an encrypted list had her bursting at the seams to tell someone. How could she simply ignore the message and let the powers that be sweep their dirty little secrets under a politicized rug? But who could she turn to or believe in enough to provide solid advice? Anyone could be involved in this "Association." For weeks, trust no one had been her mantra. But each passing day had her more convinced someone lurked in the shadows, watching her every move, and the paranoia smothered her with feelings of impending doom.

Fiddling with the locket around her neck, she thought about her twin…the only person Alyssa truly trusted, aside from her brother. Emily had a sixth sense that seemed to guide her decisions. She would know whether to pass along the secret list or burn it.

Several times over the last three weeks, Alyssa started to call Emily, and each time she stopped short of pushing Send. Derek taught his intern well. If "The Association" tailed Alyssa, her phone would likely be bugged, too. The thought of putting her twin in danger clamped Alyssa's stomach like a coiling snake squeezing until she couldn't breathe. A letter sent from a random mail drop would go undetected. She'd wait until the two could meet. In the meantime, Alyssa would lay low, do her job, and avoid confrontation.

Glancing at her watch, she realized the late hour. Another workday drew to an end, and she'd need to rush if she wanted to catch her train home. Exiting at the rear of the Capitol Rotunda, she again tightened the grasp on her coat collar, wishing she'd remembered to grab the blue and white scarf she usually wore on windy mornings. The chill within her deepened as she strode the same route, she had walked every day for the past year. West on Independence to the L'Enfant Plaza Metro Station where she caught the Silver train line to McLean, Virginia. From there, she drove home.

Arriving just in time to catch her shuttle, she drew in a deep breath and stepped from the platform into the train. When the door closed, she squeezed her eyes tightly then released the pressure to relax the pinch twisting in the back of her neck. Once she knew Emily received her message, Alyssa felt sure together they could devise a plan to end her nightmare. She leaned back in her seat deep in thought, feeling thankful she survived another day—looking past a dark, hooded figure hunched only a few seats away.

The List—Alyssa's Revenge

Book 2—Deep State Mysteries

Print and Audible Versions Available

USA Today Bestselling Author, Casi McLean's new Deep State Mystery, The List—Alyssa's Revenge, is a fast paced, cross-genre novel that combines supernatural, romantic suspense, and an NCIS mystery into a stunning thriller. Evil oozes from the pages as she takes us on an incredible journey through the underbelly of society.

When her fiancé is injured in Afghanistan, Harper Drake immerses herself in her military career. Now, as NCIS Director, she heads a secret faction, fighting corruption and terrorism—until she's abducted by a trafficking cartel.

Wyatt Rose can't overcome his loss—especially after his sister's murder. When the New Patriots recruit him, he finds a traumatized girl that spirals him down a rabbit hole of conspiracy, drug smugglers, and slavery.

Obsessed with revenge, can a ghost save Wyatt and Harper before her rage explodes, or will she spin them all through the gates of Hell?

When Revenge Sparks Danger — Karma is Hell!

★★★★★ "So many twists and subplots pepper this suspense, but they all come together into a tapestry of amazing imagination and powerful writing! Casi McLean has pulled off another genre bending tale that will draw readers in like bees to honey!" —ToMeTender Book Blog Reviews

★★★★★ "Casi McLean takes us on an incredible journey through the underbelly of society… [the reality of] a fifteen-year-old caught in the web of human trafficking… and a supernatural element I couldn't put down."—N.N. Light's Book Heaven

Excerpt

Chapter One

Hearing the doorlatch click closed, Hanna slid the handcuffs off her thin wrists, stood, then tiptoed across the cold, cement floor. She peered through the cracked window and saw him drive away.

"Is Damien gone?"

Hanna nodded then turned toward the voice.

"It's dark so make sure he's not testing us again." The young girl, still shackled to a plumbing pipe under the sink, trembled. She drew her knees to her chest then wrapped her free arm around them.

Hanna wiped a tear from her cheek, scooted across the concrete floor then knelt beside her. Yanking at the child's handcuffs, she whispered, "I don't want to leave you here."

Sarah forced a haggard smile. No longer did her eyes sparkle with the innocence of a thirteen-year-old child. Like windows into her shattered soul, her gaze seemed cold and hollow.

Hanna's heart broke every time she thought of the abuse Sarah had already survived.

When her family moved to El Paso, Texas, Sarah's shy nature left her feeling like an outsider. Her super social parents never understood why Sarah had difficulty making friends. "It's easy, Sarah. Just put yourself out there. Talk to people," her mother advised. But Sarah didn't know what to say…until Dylan caught up to her walking home one afternoon. An older boy paying attention to Sarah delighted her. Finally, someone noticed her, talked to and made her feel normal. Thrilled at the changes they saw in their daughter, her parents encouraged the friendship.

Every weekday before school, Dylan met her at the street corner and walked her to class and each afternoon he'd escort her home. Over the next few months, he charmed her, gave her thoughtful gifts, told her how beautiful she was— and said he loved her. On her birthday, he invited her to a concert at The Plaza Theater. Sarah was over the moon…but her parents weren't.

The extravagant venue made them suspicious of Dylan's intentions. After a shower of questions turned into a huge fight—resulting in a month's restriction and forbidding her from seeing Dylan--Sarah texted him, snuck out that night—and her life spun into Hell. Dylan delivered her to Diablo. Betrayed and terrified, she watched as the slave-trader dealt him $1,000 cash.

Smiling, Dylan winked. "Thanks, kiddo." Then he turned and strolled away, counting his stash.

Though Diablo held her captive for a week as they drove to Atlanta, he didn't harm her. She ate well, received nice clothes, and he never laid a hand on her.

"A lot of big-spenders will come for the Super Bowl. A blonde-haired, blue-eyed beauty like you will easily bring in $400 or more for a half hours work." He rubbed his hands together. "And a hefty profit for me." He chuckled.

Hanna had heard a similar hype from Damien, but her abduction wasn't quite as elaborately calculated. Known as Atlanta's premier shopping mall, Phipps Plaza drew high-end customers, so Hanna's parents never dreamed danger lurked in their own neighborhood. Hanna, along with Abby and Rachel, her two besties, simply went to the movies on a Saturday afternoon like typical fourteen-year-old teenagers. Afterward, the girls strolled around the mall. They had just left Nordstrom's when Hanna needed to use the bathroom.

"I'm good." Abby turned to Rachel. "I'll just wander through the jewelry store if you want to go with."

"Ohhh, I love that store. You go ahead, Hanna. We'll hang here until you get back."

"I'll be quick." Hanna rushed past two men's shops then turned left down a short hallway to the ladies' room. Who would have thought that single decision would change her life forever?

At first glance, the bathroom appeared empty. She never saw the man hiding in the stall. Once she finished her business, she placed her purse on the counter and washed her hands then turned to grab a paper towel. A heartbeat later, a hand slid around her waist and another cupped over her mouth and nose with a cloth that smelled like the worms in her biology class. She squirmed, kicked, and tried to bite him until everything went black.

She woke up with a headache, cuffed to a bed in a hotel room, a swatch of duct tape stuck to her mouth. Kidnapped December 28th, she'd been with Damien ever since. Hanna wasn't sure what day of the week it was today, let alone the date, but she knew the month…December. She could scarcely believe she'd lived in his stable for two years. But she'd never forget the day she disappeared…only three days after Christmas. Had her parents searched for her? Had they given up? How many times had she wondered how long Abby and Rachel waited before looking for her? Did they find her purse…how had they told her parents?

After the Super Bowl, Damien moved all his "children" to the Washington D.C. suburbs. McLean, Virginia to be precise, where the CIA's main offices reside. All summer, Damien hid his stable right under their noses. Now, paired two to a room, his victims resided, cuffed inside their prison in the basement of a boathouse. Closed for the season, the abandoned facility lay beneath an expressway bridge, where no one would hear their cries for help. It mattered little where the stable relocated. Damien auctioned his young boys and girls on the dark web to the highest local bidders. Diablo hadn't lied when he told Sarah her services would go for four-hundred dollars or more per half hour. Damien must have raked in a fortune.

Hanna shook her head and brushed away a random tear trickling down her cheek. "Try again, Sarah. Squeeze your hand as small as you can…like this." Holding out her palm, she maneuvered her thumb toward her pinky until the joint popped. "That's right." She snatched the handcuffs and held them firm. "Now pull…harder…harder."

Tears streaming, Sarah tried again with no results. "My fingers can't do that." She yanked and tugged at the cuffs then shook her head. "It's no use. I can't get loose and it hurts when I try to fold my hand like yours."

Hanna frowned. "As much as he hurts you?"

She shook her head and tried again. "I can't get free. You've got to go, now, Hanna. Before he comes back. You can get help and bring the police here."

"But Damien said if one of us leaves, he'd kill the one left behind. You've got to come with me."

"If you don't find help, we'll stay imprisoned in this Hell forever. You are our only chance to escape." She offered a pleading expression. "You'll come back for me. I promise I'll stay alive until you do." She held out her pinky toward Hanna. "Sister's forever?"

Throat burning at the thought of leaving Sarah behind, Hanna linked her little finger with Sarah's. "Sister's forever." She gave her a long, tight hug then returned to the window. Blinking back watering eyes, she peered outside. Seeing no one, she took off her shirt and wrapped it around her fist then turned to Sarah. "You'll be colder with the window broken."

"I know. We talked about this. I'll be fine. Hurry now."

Hanna averted her eyes to protect them from the shattering glass then slammed her fist into the window. The crack gave way, spitting splinters everywhere. She pressed against the lingering shards to break off the jagged glass then draped her tee-shirt over the rough edges and hoisted her body up and over the casing before sliding to the ground outside. Free…she was free…but for how long? She yanked her shirt from the window, shook it several times then put it on. Tiny slivers still bit her back, but she was free…that's all that mattered. Barefoot, she made her way across the boatyard. Canoes and kayaks lined the shore, all fastened securely.

Moonbeams reflecting off the river twinkled like stars. She gazed across the water and saw in the distance, a stream of headlights racing through the night. A highway? To her right, a large bridge forged across the Potomac, and to the left, a canal lined by a path reached into the darkness beyond.

A car slowed in front of the building, and Hanna's attention flew into alert. She dropped to the ground and crawled until she slipped around the side. Cautiously, she edged closer to the river then crouched next to a stone structure decorated with graffiti. Trembling from both the cold and fear, she slid into the brush then curled into a ball and prayed. *Dear Father in Heaven…please help me…help me save Sarah.* Lowering her head, she finally let her pent-up tears escape.

"Don't cry, sweetie."

Cowering, Hanna snapped around, her arms shielding her face from the beating she knew came next.

"I won't hurt you."

The voice sounded so gentle and sincere. Hanna lowered her arms, eyes still squeezed shut, she pried them open a slit to see a beautiful woman kneeling beside her. "Who are you?"

"I saw you scurrying across the boatyard, looking as if you needed help." She held out an arm, hand splayed toward Hanna. "What's your name?"

Cautiously, she glanced around, searching for Damien or any potential threat, then timidly reached for the woman's arm. "Hanna."

"That's a lovely name. Is someone chasing you? Are you running away? You look terrified."

The woman's long dark hair reminded Hanna of dark chocolate, a pleasant memory she hadn't thought about in a long time. "Why are you wandering outside so late at night and all alone?"

The woman chuckled. "I was about to ask you the same question. If you're in danger, please, let me help you." She grasped Hanna's wrist and tugged, drawing her from her hiding place.

Her first instinct was to run…but how far could she go, barefoot and dressed in nothing more than one of Damien's huge tee-shirts? Keeping his stable two to a room, shoeless, and scantily dressed was one more trick he used to make sure they stayed put.

Hanna eyed the woman with a scrutinizing glare. Where had she come from? No one had been lurking around the boatyard, had they? Again, she questioned her own instincts.

"You're trembling." The woman rubbed her hands over Hanna's upper arms. "You're running from someone, am I right? Someone who's hurt you?"

She nodded. "He has my sister locked away. He'll kill her if I don't find help soon." Hanna shifted her gaze to the building now about one hundred yards away, then again to the woman. "I don't think you and I alone could rescue my sister. Can you take me to the police...or call 911 on your cell phone?"

"I know it sounds lame, but I lost my cell phone in the river, and I'm abandoned here with no car either...but here" —she took off her royal blue coat and draped it over Hanna's shoulders— "take my wrap. It will keep you warm until you find someone to help you."

"No, I couldn't take your coat. You're stranded here in the cold, too."

"I insist." The woman placed her palms on Hanna's shoulders. "I'll be fine, and you will too if you do exactly as I say. Do you think you can do that?"

Again, she nodded, hope rising.

"Go behind the building there, where you see the canoes." She pointed.

"No." Hanna shrank away. "That's where Damien is. I can't go back there."

"You can, and you will, for your sister's sake if not your own, you must trust me."

"But you don't understand. I—"

The woman's expression softened, and she squeezed Hanna's hand. "I understand so much more than you know. I will get you the help you need, but you must follow my instructions precisely. Can you do that?"

Pausing, she considered her options. The woman's voice, so steady, strong, and confident, Hanna wasn't sure why, but she did trust her. Slowly, Hanna nodded.

"Good. Now, you see the clump of trees by the shore just beyond the rows of boats?"

Stretching her neck, she peered around the kayaks and canoes. "Yes. I see them, but—"

"When you get there, you'll find an untethered canoe floating in the weeds. Get into the boat and push off the shore. The current will take you to safety."

"How do you know? I can't see a thing from here and if I go back to the boathouse, Damien will kill me and maybe come searching for you, too." She couldn't stop shivering now, dreading what that terrible man would do to her.

"Don't worry about me. Think about you and your sister. Now go. Hurry. Crouch down in the canoe until you hit land. You'll find help there, I promise."

Hanna turned and ran then halted. Looking over her shoulder, she briefly pressed her lips together then spoke softly. "I don't even know your name."

The woman smiled. "Alyssa…"

"Thank you…Alyssa." She turned and sprinted as fast as her bare feet would allow toward the clump of trees.

Virtually Timeless

From USA Today Bestselling Author, Casi McLean, comes a gripping techno-thriller, part of a multi-author series tied together by an interlocking cast of characters, all centered around the fantastic new promise of high technology and the endless possibilities for crime that technology offers, in a world where getting away with murder can be not only plausible, but easy...if you just know how.

Another gripping thriller from Casi McLean, Virtually Timeless casts a fascinating spin on crime suspense.

When Atlanta-based twins, Sydney and Noah Monaco, mysteriously inherit property eight-hundred miles away, their curiosity prompts them to investigate the bequest.

Noah flies to Connecticut to check out the estate and stumbles upon a confused woman wandering through the forest. His medical instincts kick-in but helping her spirals him into the crosshairs of dangerous criminals out for revenge.

When he fails to connect at the specified time, Sydney's private-eye impulse slides into gear. She finds her brother, but the search exposes a hidden chamber, an ancient artifact, and a decade-old crime, thrusting them down a rabbit-hole of mayhem, medical mystery, and murder.

To solve the case, characters from other volumes of this high-tech series come in to lend a hand. In order to get answers before the villains catch up to them, the twins must use cutting-edge technology to unravel the mysteries before the murderers strike again.

★★★★★ "So many twists and subplots pepper this suspense thriller, but they all come together into a tapestry of amazing imagination and powerful writing! Casi McLean has pulled off another genre bending tale that will draw readers in like bees to honey!"

Excerpt

Chapter 1

The first scream, masked by the splashing streams of Indian Lake Creek tumbling over rocky falls, sounded like an injured animal. A bobcat perhaps, calling her mate? Noah dismissed the squeal and continued his hike through the autumn-swept forest. The second scream spiked his pulse and his medical instinct snapped to alert. The eerie cry sent a chill down his spine, causing tiny hairs on the back of his neck to rise. Definitely human, and female, the shriek shattered the silence with piercing terror.

Darting through the woods toward her wails, he took care to stay on what paths he could, making as little noise approaching as possible. Whatever—or whoever—caused the victim's cries might mean danger for Noah as well as the girl. Wild animals often attacked when injured. He challenged his memory to recall what potentially dangerous creatures inhabited the New England and Hudson Valley forests.

Slowing his pace as the creekbank came into view, he edged closer. Hearing the girl's muffled anguish, he nixed the animal idea, envisioning instead a hand covering her mouth. Thrashing sounds against the ground told him she struggled to escape. Noah slid behind a mass of dense foliage then craned his neck to see around the trunk of a red oak tree.

A stocky man with dirty-blond hair flaring beneath a navy-blue baseball cap sat over the girl's thighs. His back to Noah, the man leaned forward, causing his slate-gray sweatshirt to ride upward enough to reveal a gun stuffed into the waistband of his blue jeans. He angled his head then puffed a breathy whisper into her face.

With a sour expression pinching her nose and lips, the young woman jerked and twisted her face away from his.

"You're a feisty little bitch. I'll give you that." The thug forced her wrists against the dirt then, placing a knee on her forearm, he grabbed a fistful of her T-shirt at the neck and yanked until the fabric ripped, exposing a bare breast.

"Stop. Let…go…of…me." Kicking and squirming, she twisted her torso, lunging her body to force him off balance, but her waning strength couldn't counter his weight. The man easily dominated her frail frame and laughed at her feeble attempts.

Believing the girl had little chance of survival if the guy pulled his gun, Noah had to act now. Any chance he had of helping her escape—of saving her life—had to occur now, while the thug was distracted. What could he do to stop the assault…maybe catch the assailant off guard? Adrenaline feeding his emotion, he aimed his gaze along the shoreline searching for something— anything he could use to overtake the man. Seeing nothing helpful, aside from a few rocks, he stiffened as a shot of adrenaline slithered around his spine, tightening the knot already coiled in his stomach. On impulse, he shoved aside branches, shooting through the brush onto the creekbank then dashed toward the skirmish.

When the girl caught a glimpse of him sprinting forward, her eyes went wide.

With reckless abandon, he dove onto the man's back… snatched the gun then rolled on his side and snapped up on one knee. He pointed the firearm with a firm arm in a stance he'd only seen on television. Feeling like a character on *NCIS*, he shouted a command. "Get the hell off of her." Hands locked on the gun with a death grip, he slowly stood.

Immediately, the man raised his hands in the air, straightened his back, then stepped to the side. "No need to get excited, buddy."

Noah hitched the gun slightly to his right, indicating a clearing to which the man responded by taking several steps backward. *God, what the hell should he do now? He'd never so much as held a gun before, let alone threatened a man's life. The Hippocratic Oath he vowed shot through his spinning thoughts… First, do no harm.*

Gun aimed at the attacker, he glanced at the girl and briefly assessed the extent of her injuries. A bloody lip… an oozing gash on the side of her left eye… and a few contusions on her shoulder and neck.

Drawing her elbows inside the ripped shirt, she shifted around the torn side to her back then slid her arms into the sleeves.

Hmm, smart. Noah turned his head to check on the man then returned his gaze to the woman. "Are you okay?"

She stood, quickly inspecting herself. "I think so." After brushing the dirt from her clothes, she shifted her gaze back to Noah.

He cocked his head toward her attacker. "Do you know this guy?"

She shot a glance in the man's direction then shook her head.

Noah dug into his pocket for his phone. After hiking this property off and on for the last twenty-four hours, he knew cell service was spotty. Clicking his smartphone open, he touched the screen, pressed 911, then held the device to his ear.

"No need to call the cops, man." The culprit frowned and slightly lowered his hands as he took a step forward.

"Don't even think of it." Noah flicked the gun tip, motioning for the man to back off. When the phone call failed, he feigned a connection. He had no intention of letting a criminal know how vulnerable he was. "Yes. This is Doctor Noah Monaco. I'd like to report an...incident. I was walking my property and came across a fella attacking a young woman. I'm holding him at gunpoint...about a mile off route seven north of Sharon. 5720... toward the rear of the property by the Indian Lake Creek. Thank you." He lifted his gaze to meet the thug. "You might as well have a seat. We have a few minutes before the police arrive."

The man huffed. "I'm good. If you'd let me explain—"

"I'm not interested in your explanation. Save that for the police." Taking sidelong glances toward the victim, he held the gun firmly aimed. Something about this woman intrigued him. Her jeans hung loose on her slight frame, and her T-shirt now draped off one shoulder, swallowed her. Tousled locks of long blonde hair caught glints of sunlight that almost sparkled when she moved. Her face, though pretty, was drawn and her blank expressions puzzled Noah. Did she not understand the situation? He softened his tone. "Your forehead and lip are bleeding."

Again, she offered him a blank stare. Her hand shot to her head. Touching the gash, she winced then dropped her hand and stared at the blood on her palm.

"I'm a doctor. If it's okay with you, I'll take a look at your injury." He watched her expression closely. The normal reaction he expected never surfaced. Perhaps the incident traumatized her more than she let on?

"Did you shoot me?" Taking a few steps backward, she glared at Noah.

"No. I would never... that man attacked you." He pointed toward the clearing. "I heard your screams and came to your rescue. I can only imagine what that creep had in mind, but—" He stopped mid-sentence and observed her movements.

Keeping her eyes fixed on Noah, she turned her head, shot a quick glance then returned her stare. "What man?"

Snapping a gaze to his right, he followed the direction of his outstretched arm...his hand still clutching the gun aimed at the criminal. But the man had vanished. Damn. Noah was so distracted by the young woman's wounds, he didn't notice the man disappear into the forest. Should he follow him or tend to the woman? Even if he caught up to the thug, what would he do? Shoot him? No. To hell with the criminal. The girl needed Noah's help. Dropping his arm, he returned his gaze to the woman just in time to see her disappear into the woods.

What the hell was going on? Concerned about her wounds, Noah took off after her. After stuffing his phone into his back-left pocket, he shoved the gun into the right then picked up speed. He could hear her footsteps crackling through the underbrush and saw an occasional flash of her blonde hair as she whipped back and forth between the trees. When she chose the mountain trail over the creek, he quietly cussed himself for letting up on his treadmill workouts. For such a frail-looking girl, her energy surprised him.

At the top of the trail, the pathway split. She veered left and he followed suit, sprinting where he could in order to catch up. Gaze fixed on her, Noah strode forward... until his feet met only air. The force behind his pace propelled him forward... rolling... spinning... colliding with everything in his path until his head hit the side of a tree. The sunshine dimmed to tiny pinholes of light... then faded into a black abyss..

A Switch In Time—The President Is Missing

Print and Audible Versions Available

A note from the author: My mother, Eleanor LaRue, initially wrote this manuscript in 1960 but never had it published...she left it to me when she passed away in 1995...**BEFORE** I began writing. I found the story when I moved a few years ago and felt compelled to bring her story to life. Over the last two years, I've updated, edited, tweaked, and added a time travel element for a contemporary spin. My mom lived decades before her time, but her message is as significant today as it was in 1960. Thank you for reading our novel!

Description

USA Today Bestselling Author, Casi McLean, presents A Switch In Time—a gripping time slip thriller ripped from today's headlines.
In a country divided, where terrorists hijack peaceful protests and threaten the fabric of America's democracy, President Emery Clayton, III discovers a global power behind the insurrection. He escapes to the White House attic to plan a counterblow, steering clear of initiating World War III—and vanishes.

After years of studying to realize his dream, James Rucker's future explodes when he's falsely accused of cheating on his final exams. Vowing he's had enough, he joins a civil rights movement. But his trip to connect with the anarchists stops cold when his flight is struck by lightning and plummets into the ocean.

Can one man's soul rip through time to a different era…survive a plane crash…and mitigate a broken man's rage in time to save his own nation from total destruction?

★★★★★ "Casi McLean takes us on an incredible journey through the underbelly of society with a premise ripped from today's headlines. A gripping political thriller." —N.N. Light's Book Heaven

Preface

"Those who control the present, control the past and those who control the past, control the future."

George Orwell's—1984

Present Day

Emery Clayton peered through a dusty windowpane unnoticed from the grounds below. He could almost hear the whispers of those who strode before him. Hidden behind storage closets and nestled beneath the sloped ceiling on the north side of the White House, this secluded attic chamber offered the president a secret refuge to escape the bustling activity of the halls below. Emery might never have found the room himself, had he not searched for a quiet spot away from the madding crowd.

For the last three years, he found solace within this secret space…a place to think and sort through the dissidence running rampant in the America he so dearly loved. As President, he straddled the pinnacle of a double-edged sword threatening the fabric of the nation's democracy.

Dropping his gaze, he turned and paced toward an old wooden secretary. No longer did the Resolute Desk sit with pride in the Oval Office. Cast aside in a forgotten room by his predecessors, the oak treasure, an 1880 gift from Queen Victoria, now gathered dust and cobwebs, a powerless image of a shattered country. Pondering how he'd heal the polarized Congress and divided population paralyzing the nation, he resolved to unite America. Never would he sit idly by and watch this country wither and die.

Emery ran a palm over the smooth surface. His finger touched an etched insignia carved into the wooden drawer. Drawing his glasses from his breast pocket, he perched them on the end of his nose and read aloud the words inscribed.

"God grant me wisdom to light the way and the strength of our forefathers to save the day."

A heartbeat later, President Emery Clayton III vanished into a swirling tempest of blue haze.

Please check out my memoir
on Amazon.

Wingless Butterfly—
Healing
The Broken Child Within

A Memoir

By

Casi McLean

Thank you for reading my stories.

<u>Please consider leaving an Amazon Review.</u>

You are my inspiration.
And your support is priceless!

Casi McLean

Made in the USA
Monee, IL
05 August 2023

40507664R00125